# WINE COUNTRY COURIER
## *Community Buzz*

### GRANT ASHTON CHARGED WITH SPENCER ASHTON'S MURDER

Well, well, well. For someone so highly regarded in the community, Grant Ashton has his share of problems, yet he doesn't seem to be putting up a fight against the charges against him. This reporter even thought he'd seen resignation in Grant's eyes at the courthouse. Yet why would Grant stoop to murdering Spencer Ashton after all his family has been through? It just doesn't make any sense....

And speaking of senses... We've spotted an incredibly handsome, buff and mysterious new man in town— a true delight to the eyes.

Who is this gorgeous blue-eyed Ford Matthews? And why has he been trying to visit Grant Ashton? Rumor has it that he's been seen around town with the late Spencer Ashton's presumed mistress, Kerry Roarke. Perhaps he has something to do with the murder investigation? Only time and the ongoing family feud will reveal the truth....

Dear Reader,

Welcome to another fabulous month of novels from Silhouette Desire. Our DYNASTIES: THE ASHTONS continuity continues with Kristi Gold's *Mistaken for a Mistress*. Ford Ashton sets out to find the truth about who really murdered his grandfather and believes the answers may lie with the man's mistress—but who is Kerry Roarke *really*? *USA TODAY* bestselling author Jennifer Greene is back with a stellar novel, *Hot to the Touch*. You'll love this wounded veteran hero and the feisty female whose special touch heals him.

TEXAS CATTLEMAN'S CLUB: THE SECRET DIARY presents its second installment with *Less-than-Innocent Invitation* by Shirley Rogers. It seems this millionaire rancher has to keep tabs on his ex-girlfriend by putting her up at his Texas spread. Oh, poor girl...trapped with a sexy—wealthy—cowboy! There's a brand-new KING OF HEARTS book by Katherine Garbera as the mysterious El Rey's matchmaking attempts continue in *Rock Me All Night*. Linda Conrad begins a compelling new miniseries called THE GYPSY INHERITANCE, the first of which is *Seduction by the Book*. Look for the remaining two novels to follow in September and October. And finally, Laura Wright winds up her royal series with *Her Royal Bed*. There's lots of revenge, royalty and romance to be enjoyed.

Thanks for choosing Silhouette Desire. In the coming months be sure to look for titles by authors Peggy Moreland, Annette Broadrick and the incomparable Diana Palmer.

Happy reading!

*Melissa Jeglinski*

Melissa Jeglinski
Senior Editor
Silhouette Desire

Please address questions and book requests to:
Silhouette Reader Service
U.S.: 3010 Walden Ave., P.O. Box 1325, Buffalo, NY 14269
Canadian: P.O. Box 609, Fort Erie, Ont. L2A 5X3

# MISTAKEN FOR A MISTRESS

## Kristi Gold

Silhouette®

Desire

Published by Silhouette Books
America's Publisher of Contemporary Romance

Special thanks and acknowledgment are given to Kristi Gold for her
contribution to the DYNASTIES: THE ASHTONS series.

Many thanks to the San Francisco Area RWA for answering my call
for research assistance, particularly Laura, Cynthia, Alice and Nancy.
Your help has been invaluable to this story. To all the "Ashtons" authors,
it's been a pleasure working with you.

To Marge and Bob Smith for sitting up half the night on a porch in
Pigeon Forge, helping me brainstorm the evidence in this story.

 SILHOUETTE BOOKS

ISBN 0-373-76669-6

MISTAKEN FOR A MISTRESS

Copyright © 2005 by Harlequin Books S.A.

Visit Silhouette Books at www.eHarlequin.com

**Printed in U.S.A.**

# KRISTI GOLD

has always believed that love has remarkable healing powers and feels very fortunate to be able to weave stories of romance and commitment. Since her first Desire debuted in 2000, she's sold over twenty books to Silhouette Desire. A classic seat-of-the-pants writer, she attributes her ability to write fast to a burning need to see how the book ends.

As a bestselling author, National Readers' Choice winner and Romance Writers of America RITA® Award finalist, she's learned that although accolades are wonderful, the most cherished rewards come from personal stories shared by readers, and networking with other authors, both published and aspiring.

You can reach Kristi through her Web site at www.kristigold.com or through snail-mail at P.O. Box 9070, Waco, Texas 76714. (Please include a SASE for a response).

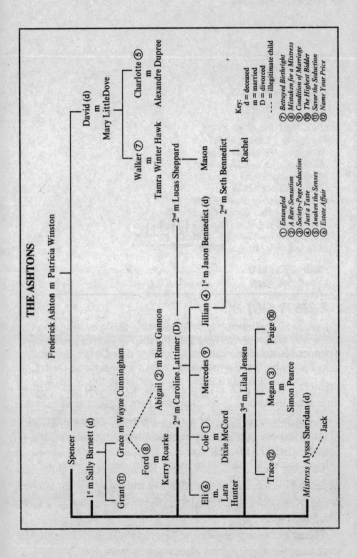

# THE ASHTONS

Frederick Ashton m Patricia Winston

Spencer

David (d) m Mary LittleDove

1st m Sally Barnett (d)

Grace m Wayne Cunningham

Abigail ② m Russ Gannon

Walker ⑦ m Tamra Winter Hawk

Charlotte ⑤ m Alexandre Dupree

Grant ⑪ m Kerry Roarke

Ford ⑧

2nd m Caroline Lattimer (D)

2nd m Lucas Sheppard

Cole ① m Dixie McCord

Mercedes ⑨

Jillian ④ 1st m Jason Bennedict (d)

Mason

2nd m Seth Bennedict

Rachel

Eli ⑥ m. Lara Hunter

3rd m Lilah Jensen

Trace ⑫

Megan ③ m Simon Pearce

Paige ⑩

Mistress Alyssa Sheridan (d)

Jack

Key:
d = deceased
m = married
D = divorced
--- = illegitimate child

① Entangled
② A Rare Sensation
③ Society-Page Seduction
④ Just a Taste
⑤ Awaken the Senses
⑥ Estate Affair
⑦ Betrayed Birthright
⑧ Mistaken for a Mistress
⑨ Condition of Marriage
⑩ The Highest Bidder
⑪ Savor the Seduction
⑫ Name Your Price

# Prologue

*San Francisco, 1991*

Sally Barnett Ashton was dead. One less complication for Spencer Ashton.

In his upscale office at Ashton-Lattimer Corporation, Spencer regarded the private investigator seated across from him, who looked as if he expected him to react with sorrow over the news of his first wife's demise. On the contrary, Spencer experienced only relief that simpering Sally was now completely out of the picture.

Leaning back in his desk chair, Spencer tented his fingers beneath his chin and prepared to ask more questions, not because he wanted to know, but because he needed to know. "And the twins?"

"They're twenty-eight now. Grant is still in Nebraska. He took over the family farm after your in-laws died."

"Former in-laws." Spencer had hated the pompous Barnetts with a passion.

The man looked somewhat put out over the comment. "Until 1975, when Sally died, they were your in-laws since you never officially divorced their daughter."

Spencer's patience was waning. "Pointless details, Rollins. Now get on with it."

"As I was saying, Grant is managing the family farm. He's turned it into a very successful crop-and-cattle venture."

Obviously the boy had inherited Spencer's business acumen, considering he was raised by a passel of country bumpkins. "What about the other one?"

The P.I. looked somewhat disgusted. "Your daughter, Grace, gave birth to two children, Ford and Abigail Ashton, in 1979 and 1981 respectively."

"Ashton?"

Rollins flipped through a folder containing the report. "Yeah. There's no marriage of record. According to the grapevine in your old hometown, she never named any father."

Spencer's anger threatened beneath the surface of his calm facade, and not because his daughter had made a presumed moral misjudgment by giving birth to two bastards. His anger stemmed from having been forced to marry the town prude in order to give his brats a name, and now his own offspring had not been held to the same standards. But he wasn't surprised. Sally had spoiled her from the day she was born. He could still remember Grace's constant wailing as an infant, even if it had been years since he'd taken off and never looked back. "Where is Grace now?"

Rollins streaked a hand over his chin. "That's a good question. She reportedly ran off with some kind of salesman about five years ago when the kids were barely in grade school. I couldn't find a trace of her, but I can keep looking."

"That won't be necessary." As long as she wasn't bugging Spencer, he didn't give a damn where she was. "What about her kids?"

"Your son is now legal guardian of your grandchildren. He's raising them alone."

Spencer found it somewhat ironic that he had other children the same age as his grandchildren. That wouldn't be unusual for a man who'd been coerced into marriage at a ridiculously young age. "Grant's not married?"

"No. Not so far."

Obviously he'd overestimated his oldest son's intelligence. Why would any man want to saddle himself with a couple of kids that weren't even his? Or any kids for that matter? He'd learned early on that child rearing should fall on women's shoulders.

Spencer sat forward and leveled a serious stare on the P.I. "When you returned to Crawley, you were discreet?"

"Of course. I told anyone who asked that I met up with you when we were both teenagers and we lost touch. I have to tell you, though. You're not very popular in town. If I were you, I wouldn't be visiting again anytime soon."

Spencer didn't intend to ever go back to godforsaken Nebraska. "And I suppose you realize that absolute discretion on your part is imperative."

"Are you referring to my knowledge that your second marriage was never valid because you never ended the first?"

True, but his marriage to his current wife was valid, not that he gave a damn about what Lilah thought about anything. She could also be replaced if necessary, and in many ways she already had. Several times. The advantages of having gullible secretaries and power. "I expect you to keep all of it to yourself. If not, you'll never work in this town again."

Rollins finally looked somewhat flustered, which pleased Spencer. "I'm a professional, Mr. Ashton. You can trust me."

Spencer trusted no one but himself. "Good. I will hold you to that."

The P.I. hesitated a moment before speaking again. "I'm no attorney, but aren't you concerned about someone finding out? And if that happens, wouldn't that mean you'd lose this company since it belonged to your second wife's father?"

"Not a concern. Her father signed his shares in this company over to me. Caroline has no claim to it." Spencer bit back a smile. What a pushover old man Lattimer had been, and so had his daughter.

"I guess you have all the bases covered." Rollins pushed his chair back, stood and gestured toward the folder. "The details are in there, copies of birth certificates and death certificates. And a few photos I managed to come across, one in particular of your son. In case you're interested in what he might look like now."

Spencer was curious, but only mildly. "That will be all." After opening his drawer, he pulled out an envelope and handed it to the investigator. "The amount we agreed upon, in cash, plus some extra to ensure your silence."

Rollins gave him a shrewd grin. "Anytime. Enjoy your trip down memory lane."

Without even an offer of a handshake, which suited Spencer fine, the man strode to the private elevator, leaving Spencer with bits and pieces of the products of his past. After the doors closed, he turned the folder around and flipped through it, coming upon the aforementioned photo of his oldest son included with a feature article in the *Crawley Crier*. He'd received some sort of business commendation from the town known for its stupid sentimentality. A boy who appeared to be about thirteen and a girl about two years his junior flanked Grant in the photo. Decent-looking kids, as far as kids went. But with his genes, Spencer certainly wouldn't expect anything less.

Bored with the whole lot of them, he flipped the file closed, just as he had closed this chapter on his life long ago. He wouldn't have to worry that Sally might someday show up on his doorstep. Most likely, neither would his foolhardy son or his reckless daughter, and even if they did, he certainly had no intention of seeing them. As far as he was concerned, his past in Crawley was as dead as the town itself.

Spencer Ashton lived a charmed life, answering to no one, and no doubt he would continue that life for many years to come. In fact, he planned to outlive them all.

# One

**S**pencer Ashton was dead, and Grant Ashton had been charged with his murder.

For most of his life, Ford Ashton had endured being called the "illegitimate" child of a "tramp" in an unforgiving Nebraska town. He'd survived his mother's cruel indifference and eventually her abandonment. But seeing his uncle—the man who'd put his own life on hold to raise him—wearing prison-issue clothes and shackled like an animal, would go down as the worst moment of Ford's twenty-six years on earth.

Standing at the back of the San Francisco courtroom among a crush of curious onlookers, with a heavy heart and sickening anger, Ford listened as the presiding judge announced, "Remanded without bail." Driven by a strong sense of desperation and blind fury, he elbowed his way through the crowd now moving in the opposite direction. Before he could reach his uncle, before he could tell him how much he meant to him, armed guards steered him away. But not before Ford met Grant's gaze and saw resignation in his eyes.

He couldn't allow his uncle to give up. Not now. Not after everything they'd been through together. With hands fisted at his sides, Ford fought the urge to pound something hard with the force of his despair. Pound something until he released all his building frustration and rage over the injustice.

"Mr. Ashton."

Ford spun around toward the unfamiliar voice and confronted an equally unfamiliar man, a slick-looking young guy wearing a dark suit. No doubt, a media vulture. "I'm not answering any damn questions."

The guy pushed his glasses up the bridge of his nose. "I'm not a reporter. I'm a clerk for your uncle's attorney. If you'll follow me, someone would like to see you."

Finally Ford would get to speak with Grant. Finally he could tell him all the things he'd needed to say that had yet to be said. Without hesitation he stepped into the vestibule, glancing to his left at the mass of reporters dogging both the prosecuting and defense attorneys, held at bay by a contingent of security guards. He followed the clerk down a narrow hallway to a secluded room. When the man opened one door, Ford expected to find his uncle waiting for him. Instead, he found Caroline Sheppard—formerly Caroline Ashton—and her second oldest son, Cole, seated at a small conference table.

After the clerk said, "I'll give you some privacy," then left, Caroline rose and crossed the room, her arms held out in welcome. "I'm so sorry, Ford."

He accepted her embrace, hiding his disappointment with a reserved smile. "I'm glad you're here, Caroline."

Cole soon joined them, his hand extended. "Sorry to have

to see you again under such sorry circumstances, Ford. We weren't sure you'd make it on time with such short notice."

Ford shook Cole's hand and said, "I wasn't sure, either. I had a connection in Denver and spent the night in the terminal, then caught the first flight out this morning."

Caroline's expression showed motherly concern, something that had been totally absent in Ford's life due to his lack of a mother. "That means you haven't had any sleep, have you?"

"No, but I wouldn't have slept, anyway, after getting your message."

She gave a one-handed sweep through her short blond hair. "I'm sorry I didn't speak with you personally. I hated that you had to hear about the arrest on your voice mail, but I didn't know how to reach you."

"Don't apologize, Caroline. You had no way of knowing I was out of town on business. I am surprised Grant didn't give you my cell phone number."

Caroline sighed. "Grant didn't want me to call you at all, but I knew you'd want to know. I also knew it could hit the national news soon, and I didn't want you and Abby to learn the facts in that way."

Abby. Damn, Ford didn't look forward to telling his sister. Although his sibling was strong willed—strong, period— she was also pregnant. With twins. "It's been three months since the murder. I thought maybe they'd marked Grant off the list of suspects. What in the hell made them decide to arrest him now?"

"Aside from the argument he had with Spencer the day of the murder," Cole began, "someone's come forward claiming to have seen him enter the building a few minutes before 9 p.m., Spencer's approximate time of death. This witness picked Grant out of a lineup."

God, Ford didn't want to hear this. If only Grant had come

home to Nebraska, none of this would have happened. If only he hadn't been so damned determined to stay in San Francisco to confront his no-good father, then he'd be home right now, helping with the harvest instead of being accused of that father's murder.

One thing Ford did know—his uncle might have been harboring some serious anger, but he would never resort to killing a man, even if justified. "He didn't do it."

"We don't think he did it, either, Ford," Caroline said. "But Spencer has always left victims in his wake, so it doesn't surprise me that continued even after his death."

Spoken like one of Spencer's victims, Ford decided. Caroline had been one of many. "Do we know who this supposed witness is and why they've taken so long to speak up?"

"We don't know any real details," Cole said. "But you'll be able to meet with Grant's attorney on Monday."

That wasn't good enough for Ford. "Why Monday? Why not now?"

"He had another court appearance today, otherwise you could've spoken with him this afternoon. Unfortunately, he'll be out of town this weekend, too."

"His name is Edgar Kent and he has an excellent reputation as a criminal defense attorney," Caroline added. "I hope you don't mind that I took the liberty of hiring him."

"I don't mind. In fact, I owe you." How could he fault this woman for anything? She'd been nothing but kind since he'd met her six months ago in Napa at Abby's wedding. "When can I see Grant?"

Caroline exchanged a brief look with Cole before saying, "According to Mr. Kent, that's not going to be possible."

The urge to knock a hole in the wall revisited Ford. "Why the hell not if they intend to keep him locked up?"

"They're taking him to one of the jails that houses some

of the worst criminals," Cole said. "You'll only be able to communicate through the attorney."

Ford's anger began to build momentum, threatening the tenuous grip he had on his temper. "I can't believe they didn't allow him to post bail."

Caroline shook her head. "They consider him a flight risk because he has no ties to the community. And because he carries the Ashton name, they also believe he might have the connections and enough money to get out of the country."

Grant might have money and the Ashton name, but not once had he ever run from his responsibility. "That's ridiculous. He's never been anywhere aside from Nebraska and now California." Unlike Ford, who'd traveled abroad the year after college graduation, thanks to his uncle, and several times since, thanks to his successful business. "I can't stand the thought of him being treated like some hardened criminal."

Cole rubbed a hand over the back of his neck and lowered his eyes. "According to the state of California, he is."

The state was wrong. Dead wrong. "What happens next?"

"Kent said the case will go before a grand jury," Cole continued. "If they find the evidence is sufficient, then he'll be arraigned again and a trial date will be set. It's my understanding that process could take some time."

Time might be on Ford's side in this instance. "I'm going to clear him. Whatever it takes."

"Grant said you'd try that," Caroline said. "He also said you needed to let the police and the justice system handle it."

"Handle it?" With every ounce of his waning composure, Ford tempered his tone. "As far as they're concerned, they have their man. I'm not going to just lie down and let Grant rot in jail on the off chance they drop the charges. While I'm here, I'm going to do some digging on my own."

Cole sent him a look of understanding. "I figured you

would, and I don't blame you. I also have some information that might help you do that. It involves Spencer's administrative assistant at Ashton-Lattimer, Kerry Roarke. I saw them together in a restaurant several months ago when I was with Dixie. Maybe she knows more than she's letting on, especially since she's the one who claimed she overheard Grant threaten Spencer."

"Grant told me about that, and he also said it was true. That's why I'm not sure she'll be of any help."

Caroline wrapped one arm around her son's waist, as if she needed physical support. "Ford, we all know that Spencer has left a trail of scorned women. I've always thought that one day he would meet up with one who wouldn't tolerate his antics. Maybe Kerry Roarke is that woman."

A trail of scorned women that had included Ford's own grandmother, and Caroline. "Then you're thinking that maybe this Kerry did him in?"

"She has a solid alibi," Cole said. "Something about taking some kind of night class. But she might have hired someone to do it."

Caroline frowned. "But that would take money, and as far as I know she doesn't have any."

"I'll find out." That, and everything else he could about Kerry Roarke. "Any idea where I can locate her?"

"She still works at Ashton-Lattimer, and that's all I know," Caroline said. "Spencer's nephew, Walker, should be able to help. He was running the company until last month. Even though he was very loyal to Spencer, and not overly fond of us, he should be reasonable."

At least that was something Ford could work with. "If you can give me his number, I'll call him after I get checked into a hotel. Any suggestions on where I should stay?"

"You can stay at The Vines with us." Caroline's voice was soothing despite Ford's turmoil.

"Thanks for the offer, but Napa's too far away from San Francisco. If I'm going to check out this Roarke woman, I need to be in the city." He also needed to be close to his uncle, even if he couldn't see him.

"You're going to have to be careful, Ford," Cole said. "If she finds out you're an Ashton, she's probably not going to talk to you, especially if she's involved in some way."

"I'll handle it." And he would. He had no tolerance for women with little regard for decency. Women like his own mother who'd abandoned her kids, just like her own father had abandoned his children. Spencer Ashton might have had a reputation of being a womanizer, but it still took two to have an affair, so that made this Kerry Roarke as guilty as Ford's grandfather, even if it turned out she wasn't guilty of murder. But someone was guilty, and it wasn't Grant.

Caroline wrung her hands over and over, another sign of her distress. "Lucas and Eli send their regards. They're sorry they couldn't come but they had to stay at the winery to prepare for the crush. Jillian and Mercedes also told me to tell you they hope to see you soon, too. They just couldn't bear to be here, but they're keeping you and Grant in their thoughts."

Ford took her hands into his. "It's okay, Caroline. It would've been tough on the girls, having to confront the man accused of killing their father."

Fury flashed in Cole's eyes. "He wasn't much of a father, Ford. Not like Grant was to you. It's tough on all of us because we believe Grant's innocent, not because of Spencer's death."

Ford shook Cole's hand again. "I appreciate your support."

"Not a problem. You're family." Cole gestured toward the

door. "We can drive you to a hotel. The car's out back. Kent told us we needed to leave that way to avoid the press."

Ford definitely wanted to avoid the press, and any pictures in the paper that might identify him. If he was going to approach this Roarke women, he needed to pretend to be someone other than an Ashton.

Once they reached the door, Caroline turned to Ford and gave him a pleading look. "Please be careful, Ford."

Oh, he intended to be careful. Very careful. He also intended to clear his uncle of all charges, no matter what it might take. Even if he had to lie.

Kerry Roarke had learned one very important lesson early in life: always be wary of a man's motives.

She'd never forgotten that lesson, and some people simply didn't understand why she was so reluctant to get involved with any man. Particularly her gal pals with whom she'd spent the regular Friday-evening preweekend celebration in a trendy Nob Hill bar, listening to them drone on and on about their active sex lives and Kerry's lack thereof. As she'd told them time and again, she wasn't interested in "finding a guy," for reasons they could never understand.

They'd departed a few minutes ago to ready for their routine club hopping, leaving Kerry with the usual admonishments to get a life. They'd also left her with two top-grade condoms that they'd slipped into her purse. Condoms or not, Kerry wasn't on the prowl today, or any day for that matter. She had a career in the making and a bitter past hanging over her head.

That's why she chose to remain at the lounge, a relatively safe place to unwind. Sure, she'd been hit on by her share of businessmen who frequented the place after work, but she'd honed the art of put-downs and prudish airs. For the most part, those skills had left her out of the line of fire of most men with lust on their minds, except for one disgustingly persistent boss who was fortunately now out of the picture, God rest his demented soul.

Despite Kerry's guardedness when it came to the opposite sex, one man standing near the bar's entry, a pilsner of beer gripped in his hand, had definitely earned her interest, mainly because he stood out from the regulars. He wore a plain navy sport coat over a white tailored shirt, sans tie, like most of the bar's male patrons in attendance. But his dark jeans spanning long solid legs and his brown leather cowboy boots didn't quite add up to corporate mogul. Considering his tanned skin and sandy blond hair cut into spiky layers, he might pass as a surfer. A really, really stunning surfer. But most surfers she'd known were a little more lean. A little less buff. Buff worked for her, if she was at all interested. Which she wasn't. Not in the least. All right, perhaps a tiny bit interested, but not enough to call him over to join her for a drink.

*You need to take a few risks, Kerry....*

In an attempt to ignore her friend's unsolicited advice, and the handsome stranger, Kerry concentrated on visually tracking a drop of condensation on the glass of club soda. Still, she couldn't seem to stop the occasional need to glance at him in spite of the lack of wisdom. Yet when he pushed off the wall and headed in her direction, she gave him her complete attention.

He definitely wasn't from the city; his gait alone indicated that. In her world, most people were always in a rush, and that applied to walking, talking and working. Not this particular man. He maneuvered his way through the tables slowly, practically sauntering toward the bar. The closer he came, the taller he seemed, his confidence overt with every step he took.

Yanking herself back into reality, Kerry took a quick drink and set the glass back down. She kept her eyes lowered, as if the soggy cocktail napkin happened to be a work of art. She heard the scrape of a stool and raised her gaze to stare ahead at the collection of liquor bottles stacked on the shelves behind the bar. But in her peripheral vision, she could see that he'd taken a seat two stools down. A comfortable distance, and a definite message he wasn't seeking her out.

That should relieve her, but instead she was disappointed. Though she shouldn't be. No matter how nice looking he might be, this man was a stranger, and most strangers meant certain danger. Right now, she really needed to finish her drink, grab her purse and go home. She really needed to have some dinner and watch a classic movie with Millie, her eccentric and beloved landlady. She really needed to quit shooting the cute guy covert glances lest he catch her. At least she wasn't panting, not yet, anyway.

"Excuse me."

Kerry froze middrink, the glass gripped firmly in her hand, a very good thing, otherwise she might be wearing the remnants of her soda. She took a quick gulp then leveled her gaze on the man not quite beside her—and immediately met a cliché. Bedroom eyes. Blue, blue bedroom eyes. Eyes as brilliant as Millie's collection of Austrian crystal.

When she realized she was staring, Kerry cleared her throat in an effort to clear away the embarrassment. "Were you addressing me?"

"Yes, ma'am. Do you live here?"

A typical pickup line, aside from the ma'am part. "I'm not really into residing in bars. Too noisy."

He grinned, and Kerry nearly slid off the stool. Did he have to have dimples to match the little cleft in his chin? And did he have to have a dark shading of whiskers to match his eyelashes? Which was kind of odd considering the lightness of his hair. But she doubted his blond highlights came from a bottle. Most likely from the sun. Perhaps he was a surfer disguised as a cowboy. Probably not a first in California.

He folded his hands in front of him. Large, sturdy hands with square, blunt fingers. A man's man hands. "I meant do you live in San Francisco?"

"Yes, I do." For ten years now, many of which hadn't been all that great.

"Good. Then maybe you can help me." Fishing into his jacket's inside pocket, he pulled out a number of brochures and fanned them out in front of him on the bar. "I'm only going to be here for a couple of days, and I can't decide what I'm supposed to do first. Any suggestions?"

Oh, she had a suggestion, all right. He needed to put a bag over his head before she went blind from his sheer beauty. She could be polite without fawning over him. After all, he seemed harmless, in a risky kind of way. "Let me see what you have, there."

After gathering up the brochures, he slid onto the stool beside her, bringing with him a subtle scent of cologne. Nothing overpowering, like most men at the office. A nice clean smell somewhere between fresh cotton and cool water. Nice, very nice. And so was he when he stuck out his hand and said, "Ford Matthews."

She took his hand into hers and noticed the calluses immediately, and the strength of his grip, although it wasn't overpowering. Just firm and solid and patently masculine, as she'd expected. After he'd called her ma'am, she'd also expected a little more country in his speech but he had no real discernable accent. In fact, he sounded fairly articulate. "I'm Kerry Roarke," she said right after he released her hand.

"Nice to meet you, Kerry."

"Ford's an interesting name." But not exactly foreign to her.

"For some reason, I think I've heard it recently, although I can't remember where."

"A lot of people own one." He grinned again and streaked a hand over his chin. "I could see you in a red Mustang convertible."

"Not hardly."

"Not even when you were sixteen?"

At sixteen she'd had nothing but the clothes on her back and a huge chip on her shoulder. "I've never owned a sports car."

"Actually, neither have I. I'm more into trucks. That's the going thing where I'm from."

Kerry toyed with the disintegrating napkin beneath her glass to avoid his unbelievable eyes. "Where are you from, Ford?"

"A small town in the Midwest."

"The Midwest covers a lot of territory. What state?"

He hesitated a moment, then said, "Kansas."

That slight hesitation bothered her a bit, but then maybe he was ashamed of his roots. That she could relate to. "What do you do for a living?"

"I'm a farmer. I own a few acres cultivated in corn. A few horses and cows."

Another of Kerry's expectations met, and very refreshing. She didn't like pretentious, wealthy men in the least. "Farming must be a tough business." And the reason for his sun-burnished skin and sun-bleached hair.

"It can be tough. Long hours, but I like working the land with my own hands."

And he owned hands that looked quite skilled, probably at everything. "It sounds intriguing."

"Not really. In fact, it's pretty boring if you're not in the business. But it's a good way to make a living if things are going well."

"And you're your own boss."

"Yep, I am."

*Yep.* Another indication of his down-home heritage. "That must be nice, being your own boss. I hope to be that someday. I'm guessing you're not in town on business then."

"Nope. Just pleasure."

In Kerry's experience, when a man said "pleasure," he usually followed it with a suggestive look. Not this enigma named Ford. He seemed refreshingly real. But what he seemed and what he was could very well be two different things. She'd given up gullible when she'd learned the true definition of "the mean streets."

"What do you do for a living?" He sounded sincere, another rarity for Kerry.

"Right now I'm working in an investment banking firm. I was an executive administrative assistant, but I've recently been demoted to human resources, due to circumstances beyond my control."

"Did you cross the boss?"

"Actually, he died."

"What happened to him?"

"He was murdered."

If Ford was at all shocked, he didn't show it. "Did they catch the guy who did it?"

Warning bells rang out in Kerry's head. Loud ones. "Who said it was a guy?"

He shrugged. "I guess I just assumed it would be."

"You're not lying to me about being a farmer, are you?" She sent him a questioning look to match her query.

A flash of confusion crossed his face. "No, why would you think that?"

"Because for the past three months, I've been hounded by the press. And I wouldn't be surprised to learn that you're a reporter looking for information. If you are, I have nothing to say."

"I promise I'm not a reporter. Not even close." When he slid off the stool, Kerry assumed he was leaving. Instead, he pulled his wallet from his back pocket, thumbed through it then said, "Damn."

She rested her elbow on the bar and propped her chin on her hand. "Forget your credentials?"

"As a matter of fact, yeah, I did. My driver's license. I don't think the guy checking me in at the airport gave it back to me."

"That's convenient."

"Not if I want to get back home."

"I meant that's convenient, not having anything to prove who you are."

He sat back down and released a rough sigh. "I went to college and I have a business degree. I nearly flunked English twice, couldn't write a decent essay to save my life and never even considered writing for a newspaper. Nowadays, I spend a lot of my time walking through manure and talking to heifers." He grinned. "The four-legged kind, so don't think I'm making some kind of sexist comment."

His smile could wither the most stoic woman, even Kerry, and that was more than obvious when she gave him one in return. "You did clean your boots before you came in here?"

"I have on new boots, bought special for the trip. I had to drive all the way into Kansas City to get them. My hometown only has a post office and a drugstore, which also serves as the grocery store. One stoplight, and that's only been there for about five years."

He seemed genuine, but she still had questions. "You don't have three kids and a wife back home, do you?"

"No way. Slim pickin's in small towns these days."

Slim pickin's in big cities, too, Kerry thought. She studied him again and didn't see anything that would indicate he was lying. She would just have to trust her instincts on this one,

and her instincts told her he was sincere, aside from being simply sensational in the looks department. Besides, she didn't
intend to do anything but have a brief conversation before she
headed home.

"Okay. I guess you've convinced me you're not some
media hound." She gestured toward the stack of brochures.
"Now hand over the tourist stuff and I'll tell you where you
need to go." And she would definitely tell him exactly where
he could go if she found out he had been lying to her.

After he slid the brochures in her direction, she began to
eliminate them one by one. "Boring." She came to the next.
"Great, if you like crowded buses." She tossed aside another.
"Too much money." She kept going until she'd exhausted all
possibilities then handed them back to him. "None of this is
worth your while."

"Then what do you suggest?"

"Several places off the beaten path, a few of the better
tourist attractions not to be missed. The night tour of Alca-
traz is pretty interesting."

His expression went suddenly serious. "Prisons don't interest me at all."

More warning bells sounded. "You haven't been in one,
have you?"

Finally his smile returned, a guarded one. "No. But I did
have a distant cousin who did time for cattle rustling."

"People really still do that?"

"Yeah. When they're desperate."

Kerry knew all about desperation. But she didn't know
what prompted her to ask, "Have you had dinner?" Maybe
her attraction to him. Maybe her co-workers voices encouraging her to take a chance now and again. This might
be considered a colossal chance, but one she felt the need
to take.

"Nope, haven't had anything since peanuts on the airplane. Do you have any suggestions?"

"Plenty. What do you like to eat?"

"Steak."

She wrinkled her nose. Beef was by no means her favorite fare. "Since you're in town, maybe you should try something different. Something exotic."

"I can do exotic. I'm not exactly opposed to taking a few risks."

Kerry had given up risks a while back, but for some reason, this man with the sparkling blue eyes, buff body and stunning mouth had her wanting to take a few risks. Small risks, she reminded herself. Having dinner in the daylight in a crowded restaurant would meet that criteria, as long as she left him with only a handshake.

Sliding from the stool, Kerry leaned down, grabbed her purse and smoothed a hand down her skirt. "Okay, Farmer Ford, I'm going to take you to one of my favorite places for a great meal, and I'm going to give you instructions on where you should go while you're in town. As long as you're buying."

He rose from the stool and stood before her, six feet of solid, electrifying male. "That's an offer I'm not going to refuse."

That was the only offer Kerry Roarke intended to make tonight.

# Two

Ford had a plan—a chance meeting, some casual conversation, earning her trust and finding out what she knew about the murder. Except, he hadn't exactly planned on Kerry Roarke's appeal.

He would like to hog-tie Walker Ashton for not sufficiently warning him. He'd only provided the name of the bar where the office staff hung out on Fridays and a general description of Kerry—blond hair, light-colored eyes, about five-seven. He hadn't bothered to mention those eyes were a color Ford had only heard about until now—violet. He also hadn't mentioned that her hair fell to the middle of her back and that her body was anything but nondescript, even if she was hiding some serious curves beneath a conservative black jacket and skirt. And damn if she didn't have a dimple. Not dimples like his and Abby's. A Shirley Temple dimple, right in the left corner of her incredible mouth. Thanks to his sister, he'd endured hours of classic movies featuring the precocious kid, otherwise he wouldn't even know what a Shirley Temple dimple was.

All that aside, he had to admit Kerry Roarke was fairly nice to be around. Maybe too nice. He had to remember that she'd been his grandfather's premortem flavor-of-the-moment, and she could hold important information about the murder. She might even be responsible, as Cole and Caroline had suggested.

At the moment, she was holding him captive with her mouth as they dined in the high-class eatery situated in an up-scale hotel not far from his own hotel. She'd wanted to take him someplace more casual, a popular Italian grill full of people, until he'd convinced her he didn't mind paying more for some quiet. Although he'd had to tip big to get seated because of his jeans, the restaurant wasn't all that crowded and the noise wasn't at all intrusive, allowing them to hold a decent conversation. An easy conversation about nothing in particular. He'd answered her questions when she'd asked, and so far he hadn't slipped up and blown his cover. Yet.

Following a slight break in their almost nonstop dialogue, Kerry dabbed at her mouth with a napkin before regarding the remnants of his so-called dinner. "You didn't eat very much."

"I'm not as hungry as I thought." Nor did he have a fondness for French cuisine or fowl.

"You didn't like the duck." She sounded disappointed, and for some reason that bothered Ford.

He took another bite to appease her. "It's just a little rich for my taste."

Tossing her napkin aside, she sat back and folded her arms beneath her breasts. "Well, I admire you for trying the escargot, even though I warned you. Guess you learned your lesson, huh?"

Little did she know, he'd figured that out at a bistro in Paris. A little garlic and a lot of butter didn't mask what they were—

snails. A lesson he'd learned a while back. But he had a feeling keeping up the farm-boy front might be more tricky than
disguising his vast dietary experiences. So might keeping his
distance from her because, despite who she was, he couldn't
deny she was classically beautiful and damn tempting. But
until proven otherwise, she was a member of the enemy camp,
a woman who helped put his uncle behind bars. A woman who
could know important details. He had to remember that, not
only tonight but for the rest of the time he planned to spend
in her company, if his plan worked.

After pushing her plate aside, she eyed the black folder
holding the check, resting next to Ford's arm. "Do you want
to split the bill?"

"No, ma'am. I've got it." Ford took out his wallet and paid
the exorbitant total with cash, including another substantial
tip. At this rate he was going to have to find an ATM, since
he didn't dare bring out a credit card with his real name. "Are
you ready to go now?"

"Sure."

When he rounded the table and pulled her chair back, she
stared at him like he'd grown two heads. "This is rather
strange."

"What's strange?"

She accepted the hand he offered and stood. "You're a
gentleman, and that's a rare breed these days."

If she knew he'd been lying to her—about his name, the
missing driver's license, his real reasons for being in town and
being with her—she wouldn't find him gentlemanly at all.
And that was something Ford had a hard time dealing with.
His uncle had taught him that lying was one of the most dis-
honorable things a man could do, especially to a woman. He
wasn't in the habit of lying to women. Normally, he let them
know upfront he wasn't looking for a serious relationship. If

that wasn't okay with them, then he'd let them go without any argument. A lonely life at times, but he wasn't ready to settle down, and he wasn't sure he would ever be. Not if he ran the risk that he'd fall for some woman who'd get tired of living in the middle of nowhere, then take off the way his mother had.

At least that wouldn't be a problem with this particular woman, he thought as they headed out of the hotel. As soon as he got what he needed from Kerry Roarke, he would walk away.

"Do you want to walk awhile?" Kerry asked after they moved through the sliding doors and onto the sidewalk.

He paused to face her, coming in contact with those killer eyes. "You're the guide. Lead on."

"We're only going a block or so," she said as they headed up the street.

Kerry walked fast but Ford managed to keep up with her. He suspected she did everything in a rush, from talk to eat, but then, considering what he'd seen of the city that day, it seemed everyone was in a hurry. After about a block or so, she crossed the sloped street, led him into a nicely landscaped, well-lit park and showed him to a bench across from a fountain, their backs to a row of buildings, an impressive cathedral looming large in the distance. The sun had set completely, leaving the sky a hazy shade of oranges and blues. Ford settled beside her, careful to keep a decent space between them. Otherwise he might forget his goal, especially when she crossed her legs and her skirt rode up higher on her thigh. He fought the urge to stare. He fought even harder the temptation to touch.

She sat back and sighed. "I love this place in the evening, especially all the people. Take that woman across the way, walking her dog."

Reluctantly he turned his attention from Kerry's legs to an elderly lady wearing an odd, flower-bedecked hat and gloves, her prissy four-legged hairball sporting a diamond-studded collar. "That's pretty interesting." And not so unlike some of the snooty women in Crawley, at least as far as the hat and attitude went.

"I guess San Francisco might seem strange to someone who lives on a farm," Kerry said. "All of the chaos and eccentrics."

"Yeah. I'm not used to seeing so many people milling around." Somewhat of a lie since he'd seen his share of big cities in the process of hawking his patented livestock feed to various companies. But he wasn't going to tell her any of that, especially since she'd told him several times at dinner how she appreciated spending time with a "common farmer." True, he had the soul of a farmer, but he had a bank account that far exceeded most men who made a living off the land.

He shifted to face her and laid an arm over the back of the bench, fighting the urge to touch that incredible fall of blond hair. "Do you like living here?"

"Sure. It's an exciting place." She turned those violet eyes on him again. "And some might say it's romantic, although I can't speak from personal experience."

Ford's experience had been limited lately too. Three months had passed since he'd visited a "special" female friend in Lincoln. A month ago, she'd moved to Chicago, and Ford had moved into celibacy, but not by choice. "Sounds like the perfect place to live if you're into that sort of thing."

She lifted one shoulder in a shrug. "Like every other big city, it has its downside."

Ford noted the weariness in her tone, as if she'd personally experienced that downside. A good lead-in. "I imagine it does, especially if you can't go to work without worrying about your boss being murdered."

"Honestly, he wasn't necessarily a nice man. Charming on the surface, but he tended to use that, and money, to get what he wanted. That's why I'm not surprised someone got tired of it and took matters into their own hands."

But was that someone her? Ford couldn't imagine that any woman with such an angelic face and pleasant disposition could actually be involved in a murder. Yet she'd basically echoed exactly what Caroline had said about Spencer. Someone had grown tired of his treachery and had done something about it. "Do they know who did it?"

"They've arrested his son." She crossed her arms beneath her breasts and stared straight head. "Can we talk about something else?"

"No problem." As far as Ford was concerned, they had plenty of time to get into that. "What do you want to talk about?"

"We could discuss what we originally intended to discuss, your tour of the city. I need to know your starting point, so where are you staying?"

Ford hooked a thumb over his shoulder. "We passed it back there. The Royalbrook Hotel."

She looked surprised. "That's a ritzy place for someone on a tight budget."

"Well, I don't get out all that much, so I decided to go for broke and stay at the best. I even have a suite with a couple of couches and one of those minibars. Damnedest thing I've ever seen." More lies. Ford had stayed in many hotel suites with minibars. And Cole had directed him to the hotel because of the proximity to the financial district, and the Ashton-Lattimer offices. Money wasn't an issue.

Kerry toyed with the hem of her skirt, drawing Ford's immediate attention. "I guess a suite might come in handy, in case you meet an interesting woman you'd like to entertain."

"I've already met one." And that was the absolute truth.

Even in the limited light, he could see a blush on her cheeks, making her all the more pretty. "I don't know how interesting I am, but I do know the city like the back of my hand. The good, the not so good, and the ugly." She lowered her gaze to her lap. "Since tomorrow's Saturday, maybe I could be your personal tour guide."

The plan was now in place, and better still, it was her idea. "I could go for that in a heartbeat. If you're not going to upset some boyfriend."

"I don't have a boyfriend, so that's not a problem."

A good thing, Ford decided. But his attraction to her wasn't good at all. It was hazardous. He would just have to keep his urges in check and a firm grip on his control and goal. "What time do you want to meet up?"

"How about 9 a.m.? I'll pick you up in front of the hotel."

"In a car?"

She smiled. "I don't think I want to carry you on my back up and down the streets of San Francisco."

Ford laughed, all the while thinking he'd like to carry her to bed. Another hazardous thought. "Okay, 9 a.m. in front of the hotel."

She secured her purse strap over her shoulder. "Great. Now that that's settled, I should be going home."

"Where is home?"

She pointed in the direction opposite the hotel. "That way."

"Where's your car?"

"I'm on foot. The parking downtown is ridiculous, and public transportation's readily available and cheap. But I can walk home from here."

They stood at the same time, coming into close enough contact to make Ford more than uncomfortable. "I can walk you home."

"That's not necessary. It's not that far, and the area is fairly safe."

"That may be, but where I come from, men escort women to their doorstep."

She straightened the lapels on his jacket. "But I'm not a defenseless woman, Ford Matthews. In fact, I'm a lot tougher than I seem."

Maybe even tough enough to have had her boss killed. She might be that tough, but right now Ford was having a huge moment of weakness, especially when she wet her lips. "Guess I'm going to have to behave myself so I don't give you a reason to slug me."

"I wouldn't necessarily slug you if you misbehaved a little."

"Oh, yeah?"

She moved closer until very little space separated them. "Nothing too naughty, of course."

Ford was having some fairly "naughty" thoughts at the moment. In fact, they could be deemed as downright dirty. Right now he really wanted to kiss her, but he realized the lack of good judgment in that. Obviously, Kerry didn't, because before Ford could brace himself, she wrapped one slender hand around his neck and brought his mouth to hers.

He'd never refused a kiss from a beautiful woman before, and he sure as hell had no desire to do that right now. Not when her sinful lips contrasted with her angelic face. Not when he could no longer resist wrapping his arms around her and pulling her against him. Not even when the kiss took on a definite wildness, growing deeper and deeper with every passing moment.

Kerry pulled away first and touched her fingertips to her lips, her blush a deeper shade of pink. "I'm sorry. I guess I got a little carried away."

If she only knew what was stirring below his belt, she'd

realize she wasn't alone. "I'm not sorry at all." Another truth among the lies, but he had to keep a tight rein on reality, and that meant not getting totally caught in her web.

She released a small, self-conscious laugh. "Just so you know, I don't normally behave that way. I've never kissed anyone I've just met. I've never wanted to."

Ford couldn't say the same thing, another fact he decided to keep to himself in a long line of many. "We'll just chalk it up to the moonlight."

She studied the darkening hazy sky. "I don't see any moon."

He took a moment to admire her, and found himself wishing things were different. Wishing they had met under different circumstances, and that she was all she appeared to be—a gorgeous woman, fresh and unassuming. And incapable of being a mistress or a murderer. "Maybe it's not out yet."

She settled her gaze on his. "Maybe it will be out tomorrow night."

Knowing she planned to spend that much time with him pleased Ford, but not for the reasons it should. "I'll see you tomorrow."

"Nine o'clock sharp," she said as she began backing away.

He slipped his hands in the pockets of his jeans. "Are you sure you don't want me to escort you home?"

She paused on the walkway, the fountain behind her providing a nice backdrop for her beauty. "I really don't think that's a good idea."

"Why's that?"

"Because I might ask you to come in, and something tells me that might be dangerous."

With that, she walked away, leaving Ford frozen where he stood as he watched the sway of her hips. No doubt danger lurked around every curve, especially hers. If he had walked her home and she had asked him in, he wasn't sure what he might have done. Probably nothing that would be considered sensible.

When she was no longer in sight, Ford left the park for the hotel. He had a lot to think about tonight, and a few things to do, namely call home. After that, he'd take a shower and go to bed in order to be well rested for his excursion with Kerry Roarke. And he suspected that prospect could very well keep him up all night.

Kerry closed the front door behind her and fell back against it. If luck prevailed, Millie might already be in bed. Otherwise, she could be in for questions she didn't want to answer.

"What have you been doing, young lady?"

So much for luck. Kerry strolled into the cluttered living room to find Millicent Lantry Morrow Vandiver seated in the red brocade wingback chair midmanicure, a turquoise turban wrapped around her hair to complement the matching caftan. She looked much younger than her seventy-eight years, thanks to a few facelifts that left her eyes a bit sunken, but her skin virtually wrinkle free. She was elegantly unconventional, a woman with a heart of gold who'd survived three husbands and had a penchant for picking up strays. Kerry was no exception to that, except that she'd remained with Millie much longer than most.

Tossing her purse aside, Kerry collapsed onto the weathered gold sofa that had seen its share of visitors, from out-of-work actors to persistent suitors to strung-out kids, according to its owner. She reached down and slipped off her heels, her feet greatly in need of a good soak. When she glanced up and noticed Millie was still awaiting an answer, she said, as nonchalantly as possible, "I've been out to dinner with a friend."

Millie resumed filing her nails. "You've been out kissing someone."

Momentarily stunned and speechless, Kerry gaped a good thirty seconds before she asked, "Why would you think that?"

She waved the fingernail file around like a maestro conducting an orchestra. "My dear, you have that look about you. You're veritably glowing. And your lipstick is smeared."

Kerry automatically swiped the back of her hand over her mouth. "How do you know I didn't mess it up during dinner?"

Millie set the file aside and folded her hands primly in her lap. "My angel, I have been married many times, and in love at least four times as many. I know when a woman has been keeping company with a young man."

Millie's intuition was as amazing as her youthful attitude, something Kerry had learned a long time ago. "Okay, I might have gotten a good-night kiss." In reality, she had delivered that kiss.

"Who is this young man?"

Kerry curled her legs beneath her. "Don't laugh, but he's a Midwest farmer in town on vacation. I met him tonight."

Millie looked both surprised and concerned. "You kissed a complete stranger?"

Kerry felt the beginnings of a blush. "It was only a simple kiss." Yet there had been nothing simple about it. She still felt the effects, remembered the sensations, wanted more of the same.

Pushing up from the chair, Millie crossed the room with measured steps. Kerry had noticed her frailty more and more each day, and that made her heart ache.

Millie settled in beside her on the sofa and took Kerry's hands into hers. "Kerry Ann, when you came to live with me, you were a scared child, full of anger and suspicion, and rightfully so. Since that time, you've blossomed into a more secure woman. Yet I'm concerned that you are still very vulnerable."

"What are you saying?" As if Kerry didn't know.

"I want you to open yourself to possibilities where men are concerned, but I also want you to be careful. I would hate to see you fall in love too quickly or trust too much."

"I just met him, for heaven's sake. I'm not in love with him." But she had to admit, she was very drawn to him. Almost to extremes. "Besides, he'll be leaving in a couple of days."

"Precisely, but one can make grave errors in judgment in two days' time."

Kerry pulled her hands from Millie's grasp and lowered her gaze to the miniature Buddha sitting in the middle of the coffee table. "It's not that big a deal, Millie. I'm only going to show him around tomorrow."

"Perhaps you would like me to chaperone to ensure your safety."

Wouldn't that be lovely? "That's not necessary, Millie. We'll be out in public. I'm just going to take him to a few places around town."

"He could very well try to take you a few places—none having to do with tourism."

Kerry glanced up to meet Millie's somber expression. "You haven't even met him yet."

"True, so do bring him by for afternoon tea. Unless you are otherwise occupied, or fear that I might steal him away."

Kerry smiled in response to Millie's sudden mischievous grin. "Actually, that could be a problem with your charm and his incredible looks."

"Then he is handsome?"

Oh, yes. "You could say that."

"I will have to judge for myself, and suppose I will have to trust your judgment, as well." She pushed off the sofa and faced Kerry. "Now I'm going upstairs since it's getting late."

"I'll be up in a minute to brush your hair." Something

Kerry had done for the past ten years for her mentor, such a small gesture in light of everything Millie had done for her.

Millie waved her hand in a dismissive gesture. "That won't be necessary, darling. You must get your rest tonight and prepare for your day tomorrow. I want you to be totally cognizant of your actions."

After Millie headed away to make the slow journey up the stairs, Kerry remained on the sofa and pondered Millie's words. Maybe she was being foolish. Maybe she was taking too big a chance. But in her heart of hearts she truly believed she could trust Ford Matthews.

Ford sensed Kerry was beginning to trust him, and although that's exactly what he'd planned, he was also beginning to feel like a jerk. But he still had to remember what he hoped to accomplish. Losing control wasn't a part of the scheme, although that's exactly what he had almost done when she'd kissed him.

Tomorrow he would take it easy with her. He'd spend the time necessary to get her to talk to him about the murder. Beyond that, he couldn't allow anything else to happen between them.

But hell, he wanted to kiss her again. He wanted to do a lot more than that.

Right now he needed to call home. Grabbing the tableside phone, Ford pounded out the number and waited, hoping his brother-in-law answered and not his sister. Chances were, Abby had spent a good part of her day fuming since he'd spoken to her husband before he'd left the hotel instead of her.

"Speak."

Damn, for once he'd lucked out. "Hey, Russ. How's it going?"

"If you mean how's your sister, I'm going to let her answer that."

"Wait a minute, I need to talk to you before—"

"Ford Ashton, you are in so much trouble you're going to need a backhoe to dig out of it."

And she would be driving the backhoe, heading straight for him. "Good evening to you, too, sis."

"Why haven't you called before now? I've been sitting here, waiting to hear why you suddenly decided to take a trip to California."

Obviously, the story hadn't made the local news out of North Platte, and cable TV was a nonentity in Crawley. Maybe this time that was a blessing. At least he could break it to her gently. "They had Grant's bail hearing today."

She drew in a harsh breath. "Bail hearing? They've arrested him?"

"Yeah, and the worst part is, they're going to keep him in jail until the trial. They're afraid he's going to skip out."

"Oh, God. Did you talk to him?"

"No. He's not allowed any visitors."

"This is insane! Uncle Grant couldn't have done this."

He hated hearing Abby so upset, especially because of the pregnancy. He knew enough to know that carrying twins was risky enough without emotional stress. "Calm down, Abby. I'm going to clear him of the charges if it's the last thing I do."

"How are you going to do that?"

He explained Kerry's affiliation with Spencer before launching into his plan to garner information from her. When he was finished, Abby asked, "Is she pretty?"

Pretty wasn't the half of it. "Yeah, she is."

"Oh, wonderful. I hope you keep your little brain from taking over your big brain."

"Not funny, Abby. This is serious business. I'm seeing her to get information, not to seduce her. Besides, so far she seems fairly nice." Very nice, unpretentious, and that's what bugged Ford the most. Maybe everyone had been wrong about her.

"You know something, Ford? Maybe you *should* seduce her, if that's the only way you can get information."

"You don't mean that, Abby."

"Normally I wouldn't even consider such a thing. But if this woman is responsible for the murder, or if she's protecting the real killer, then I say you pull out all the stops and do what you have to do. This is Grant's life we're talking about here. Literally. He could receive the maximum penalty for something he didn't do."

He could be executed, what Abby had failed to say, but Ford got her meaning, loud and clear. He couldn't stomach the thought of Grant suffering that fate. He couldn't stand the thought of him spending his life in jail, either.

"I agree, Abby. I intend to do whatever I can to clear him. But Grant also stressed to us the importance of honesty and respect. I'm lying to this woman, and if she's not responsible for any of it, then I'm in the wrong, and I'm going to have to live with that."

"Ford, you've always been fairly cavalier with relationships with women. Don't let this one turn your head around until you can't see straight."

At times he believed Kerry Roarke was already clouding his judgment, and he'd only known her for about five hours. Which made spending all day with her dicey. But he had no choice. "I'll do what I have to do, Abby. And if this all turns out to be a dead end, I'm not going to give up. I'll stay here until I find out who really did this and see Grant walk out of that hell-hole."

"I wish I could be there with you."

Ford hated the hint of tears in Abby's voice. Abby rarely cried, but he could understand why she would feel the need.

"You've got to think about the babies and your health, Abby. This is already stressful enough for you."

"Yes, but I'll handle it. Besides, I have Russ."

Thank God she did have Russ, and although Ford was happy she'd found a life partner, at times he envied them both. "Speaking of Russ, tell him thanks again for keeping the place in order."

"I will. Between him and Buck, everything will get done."

Thank God for Buck Collier, too. The foreman had been around for as long as Ford could remember. In many ways, he'd also served as a surrogate father. At least the men in his and Abby's lives had been great role models. "I'm going to let you go now. Try to get some rest."

"You, too, Ford. And be careful. I don't want to see you get hurt."

Hurt? Where had that come from? Ford Ashton didn't get hurt. He never allowed himself that emotion, not since the day his mother had walked out the door and never returned. He vowed he never would. "I'll be fine, Abby. And if I can find some way to get word to Grant, I'll send him your love."

"You do that. And in the meantime, call every now and then, will you?"

"I'll stay in touch when I have the chance." But tomorrow that might be impossible. Tomorrow he planned to be occupied by Kerry Roarke.

After hanging up from his sister, Ford stripped out of all of his clothes and lay across the bed, a glass half-full of mini-bar whiskey resting on his bare chest. He didn't like feeling this way, at war with his honor and, worse, battling his libido. Kerry had definitely stirred up big trouble, maybe more than he could handle. Right now he had to get a grip on some serious strength. Otherwise, their little sightseeing trip and his fact-finding expedition might get thrown over for a totally different kind of journey. One that involved a good-looking lady who could kiss way too well, and a hot-blooded man who hadn't kept company with a woman of her caliber in quite some time, if ever. A deadly combination. He'd just have to keep his head on straight.

# Three

The minute Ford walked out of the Royalbrook Hotel's revolving doors, his head started spinning. Parked in the circular drive beneath the portico sat a little red Mustang convertible with the top down. And behind the wheel of that hot little car was an equally hot blonde, her hair secured high atop her head, sunglasses concealing her eyes. But Ford remembered every detail of those eyes without having to see them this morning.

He approached the car, gave it a long glance and whistled. "Nice wheels. Mind if I come along for the ride?"

She patted the passenger seat. "Sure. Hop in. I'm in the mood for a little adventure."

Ford shouldn't be in the mood for adventure, but unfortunately, he couldn't deny that he'd looked forward to today. After seeing her dressed in a blue, sleeveless, striped top that tied at the neck and showed a lot of bare arms and back, he also couldn't deny that a strong sense of awareness had begun to surface. The solid matching skirt that came to her thighs only made matters worse, and threatened to make him forget his goal.

This whole day trip was about information, not about his attraction to Kerry Roarke. This outing served only as a means to an end, a way to obtain information that could prove his uncle innocent. That was all it was, all it should be, and nothing more.

On that thought, Ford rounded the car and climbed into the passenger side. He powered the seat back to accommodate his legs and studied her for a moment. "You told me you never owned a Mustang."

She shrugged. "I don't own it. I rented it. It's all ours until tomorrow."

Ford didn't want to consider what tomorrow might bring. He was more interested in the here and now. And her. "What's on the agenda?"

She checked her mirrors, then steered down the drive. "Just a few sights I'd like to show you in the city."

As far as he was concerned, the best sight was sitting beside him—a portrait of prime woman. "Okay. You're the tour guide."

As they began their journey, Ford learned two very important things in a brief time—San Francisco streets qualified as an amusement ride, although he didn't exactly find them amusing. And Kerry Roarke enjoyed driving fast. She skipped the infamous Lombard Street and opted to take him down a less traveled but equally crooked road—laughing all the way. She traveled through Chinatown past the open-air markets and eventually drove down California Street and into the financial district. Ford noted an immediate change in her when they passed by a historic-looking high-rise.

"That's Ashton-Lattimer," she said with a wave of her hand and a frown on her face. "My workplace."

Ford sent a cursory glance in the building's direction—the place where Spencer had been murdered. Maybe that was the reason for her sudden mood change. "Looks like it's been around for a while."

"It has, since right after the big quake."

"How long have you been there?"

"Entirely too long."

"I'm guessing you don't like your job."

They stopped for a light, her grip tight on the wheel. "Not particularly."

"You liked what you did before your boss was killed?"

"The job was fine. But as I told you last night, I can't say the same for my boss."

Ford wondered if she'd been jilted by his grandfather or just disgusted. "That must be tough, working for someone you don't like."

"I managed. And now for the best part of the tour."

Deciding to drop the subject for now, Ford sat back while Kerry took him on a scenic drive around a road that spanned the coastline. Again she resumed tour guide status, pointing out various sights in the city. But all Ford could see were the slight strands of hair raining down from her ponytail, the movement of her lips as she talked, the line of her arm and outline of breasts. Several times he had to force his gaze away from her and back on the sights.

After they'd completed the scenic drive, Kerry took him to Fisherman's Wharf where they strolled past shops concentrated in an area that was twice the size of downtown Crawley. Several times he laid a palm on the small of her back, as if they were any other couple out for a routine Saturday excursion. And several times he'd been tempted to kiss her. He definitely had to hand it to his grandfather—the lying bastard had good taste in assistants. And maybe this particular one had suffered through enough of his disregard for women that she'd taken matters into her own hands. But Kerry Roarke a murderer? He was still having one helluva time believing that, more than before.

Following an hour of acting like serious tourists, Kerry ushered Ford back into the car for a trip to Golden Gate Park. He soon found himself seated in a rowboat on an emerald-green lake, picnic basket onboard, oars in hand, facing a woman who looked every bit the celestial being. The noon sky had become overcast, causing Kerry to discard the sunglasses. Now Ford had a first-rate view of her violet eyes, and he couldn't think of anything more fatal to his control. Except when she crossed her legs and the skirt crept higher. Not to mention the view of her cleavage and breasts that he suspected were unencumbered beneath the top. If it cooled off any more, he'd probably know for sure. If he didn't cool off, he might try to find out with his hands.

Unaware of Ford's questionable thoughts, Kerry gestured to an impressive waterfall and propped the basket on her lap, preventing him from staring at her thighs. "Row over there and we can have some lunch."

Ford complied, skirting a paddleboat navigated by a teenage boy who seemed more interested in making out with his girlfriend than steering.

"Maybe someone should tell them to find a backseat," Kerry said as she spread a blue-checked tablecloth on the deck between them.

He returned her smile, although he had to force it around a vision of finding himself in the backseat of a Mustang—with her. "Yeah. Must be nice, being so young that you don't give a damn what anyone thinks."

After they pulled alongside a rock border separating the falls from the lake, Kerry pulled out two bright-pink plastic plates and handed him one. "I can't say that I've ever been quite that carefree."

"You've never necked on a paddleboat?"

"No. Have you?"

"Nope. Not too many of those in Nebraska."

"Nebraska? I thought you lived in Kansas."

Oh, hell. "I went to college in Nebraska. I was a little more daring at that age, more inclined to take risks."

Fortunately for Ford, Kerry seemed satisfied with that answer. "I'm originally from Seattle," she said as she went back to unloading the basket.

"How did you end up in San Francisco?"

"Blind luck, actually. When I decided to leave home, I got out a map, closed my eyes and pointed. San Francisco was the largest city closest to my finger."

Although she sounded amused, Ford saw a flash of pain cross her expression before she lowered her gaze. "Didn't your folks have something to say about that?"

"My mother died when I was fourteen. My dad died before I was born, in a logging accident."

"I'm sorry to hear that. Who raised you after she died?"

"My stepfather was my legal guardian, but I can't say he was all that active in my raising. He had a lot of money but very little compassion, so I got out from under his thumb as soon as I was old enough to survive on my own. He was always taking but rarely giving back. I've found that to be true with most wealthy men."

An accurate description of Spencer Ashton. But Ford wanted to tell her that not all men with means bore that label. "That must be tough, settling in a strange city, alone."

"It wasn't so tough after I met Millie."

"Millie?"

"Millicent Vandiver, my landlady. She's a former actress and very dramatic, but she has a heart of gold. She took me in and I've been with her ever since. She's the one who packed our lunch."

"You'll have to thank her for me."

"Maybe you can meet her and thank her yourself. She's quite a character." Kerry popped open one plastic container and held it out to him. "Hope you like chicken salad."

Ford reached inside the container and took two skinny finger sandwiches. "Look's fine."

Kerry took one for herself then resealed the lid. "Be glad she didn't make her usual goose liver pate." She wrinkled her nose. "I never have acquired a taste for that."

Neither had Ford. "Did she pack anything to drink?" His mouth was dry, but not from thirst. He'd had a hard time keeping his eyes off Kerry's breasts every time she leaned over to take something from the basket.

"Let's see." Again she bent forward, causing Ford to shift on the bench as she withdrew a carafe. She twisted the lid open and sniffed it. "Mimosas. Although I'm betting there's a lot more champagne than orange juice."

"It's kind of early to be indulging in alcohol." Especially if he wanted to keep his wits about him.

She poured the liquid into a blue plastic cup and handed it to him. "A big guy like you can handle one little drink."

Ford was having one hell of a time handling being so close to her. "Okay, but just one." Being close to her made him drunk enough.

They ate in silence for a time before Kerry asked, "What about your parents?"

A sorry subject he didn't really want to broach. "Both dead." As far as he was concerned, they were.

"I'm sorry we have that in common. It's tough, isn't it?"

"I did okay. My grandparents raised me." A lie since his grandmother died four years before he was born. But he didn't want to mention his uncle for fear he might slip up again.

She offered him some grapes. "Dessert?"

"No, thanks. I'm full." Another lie. Skimpy sandwiches just didn't cut it, but he could grab something later at the hotel. At the moment he envisioned grabbing Kerry at the hotel. He sat back and studied the skies, hoping to clear those images from his head. "Looks like rain."

"I know that's how it looks, but it rarely rains in August."

Right after she said it, a few drops fell from the sky. "Must be one of those rare times," Ford said.

She laughed. "I guess so."

Ford picked up one oar, prepared to head back to the rental dock, when Kerry laid a palm on his hand. "Let's stay for a while. It won't last long." She turned her face toward the graying skies the same as he had. "Besides, I love rain."

He couldn't deny that he appreciated the way she looked right then, drops of water forming on her face and tracking a path down her slender throat. He visually followed one of those drops as it disappeared beneath the knit top. As far as urges went, he had a strong one. He wanted to follow that drop's path with his mouth, trace the line with his tongue—and keep going.

Then the deluge came, hard pelting rain, yet Kerry didn't seem to care at all, unlike most of the other boaters who had long ago headed back in. Without warning, she moved beside him on the narrow bench, their thighs and arms touching. She turned her face to his, and Ford realized he was quickly approaching a point of no return, and facing plenty of regret if he gave in. He had no choice in the matter when she reached down and pulled the tablecloth out of the basket, then draped it around them like a cocoon.

She looked up at him and said, "This gives us a little protection from the elements."

Ford needed more than a flimsy tablecloth to protect him from doing something stupid. Here he was, soaked to the skin with an incredible woman, their faces only inches apart. So he did the only thing he could think to do at the moment—kiss her soundly.

He wrapped his arms around her, and she laid one hand on his thigh, her other hand sliding through the hair at his nape. The rain continued to fall, and so did Ford's conviction to avoid this very thing. He couldn't explain why he couldn't seem to get enough of her. Couldn't explain why he slid his palm up the curve of her hip. Couldn't explain why he kept going beneath her shirt to touch her waist. Her flesh was warm in contrast with the chill of the sudden wind. She was so soft against his callused hand, her tongue smooth as it moved in sync with his. A mix of instinct and need caused him to move his hand higher over her rib cage. And then she flinched.

Reality thrust Ford back into coherency and he broke the kiss. Kerry stared at him for a moment, her eyes as hazy as his brain. She touched her fingertips to her mouth, as if she didn't quite believe what they'd done. "Maybe we should go now," she said, her voice little more than a whisper.

"That's a good idea." His voice sounded gruff and slightly angry. He *was* angry—at himself.

She clutched the wrap tightly around her and glanced away, but not before he saw wariness in her eyes. If he didn't slow down, he was going to blow his plans to hell and back. Worse, he might even forget what he needed from her, and that sure as hell wasn't taking her to bed and forgetting all about Grant's predicament. "I'm sorry, Kerry. I didn't mean to—"

"Don't apologize, Ford. We're both to blame. But I just want you to know that I'm not prone to this kind of behavior."

Although he should be suspicious—especially if she had been Spencer's mistress—he sensed she was being sincere. But his instincts about women hadn't always been on target, and he couldn't afford to let down his guard. "I guess we both just got a little carried away again."

"That we did." She tossed aside the tablecloth. "Now shall I row, or would you prefer to do it?"

He only wanted to do one thing right now—kiss her again. And again. He grabbed up the oars, thinking he should pound some sense into his head. "I'll do it. Might help work off some steam."

She smiled a self-conscious smile, revealing the dimple that threatened to shred the last of Ford's sanity. "I suppose the tour is now officially over."

Ford pushed off the rocks with the oar. "I thought we might have dinner later."

"We'll have to change first since I'm wet."

He sent a long glance down her body. "I kind of like you wet."

The comment hung over them for a long span of silence until she finally said, "Then you should like me a whole lot right now."

Problem was, Ford did like her. A lot. He couldn't let that sway him. He couldn't want more from her than a few answers. But damned if he didn't.

By the time Kerry pulled up Millie's driveway, she wanted to scream. How could she have been such an idiot? And what had possessed her to toss away common sense to the point that she'd allowed Ford Matthews, a man she knew so little about, to kiss her until she'd almost completely forgotten herself? And in a rowboat, no less. At least she was thankful he'd stopped before things had gotten totally out of hand. Of course, when he'd come so close to her scar, she'd automatically tensed. An ugly reminder of her past, one she wasn't ready for him to see, or feel, just yet. But she still felt the effects of his kiss, of his touch. She also recognized he was the first man she'd trusted enough to welcome the intimacy since that one horrible experience ten years before. Unwise, probably. Unwelcome, no. In fact, she wanted more of what they'd shared today. She wanted to feel that alive again.

After putting the car in park, Kerry turned to find Ford staring at the Victorian house, surprise in his expression. "That's a pretty impressive place. Part of the tour?"

"Actually, this is where I live."

His surprise melted into shock. "You're kidding."

"No. I've been here with Millie for ten years. Her father built it after fire destroyed the original."

He skimmed a hand over his jaw. "Is it as nice inside as it outside?"

"Would you like to come in and see? I'm sure Millie would love to meet you as soon as she returns from her investment club meeting."

He glanced down at his rain-soaked jeans. "I'm not exactly presentable right now."

Millie wouldn't mind, that much Kerry knew. But she thought it might be best if they parted company for the time being since they would be alone for another hour or so. Otherwise, she might be tempted to invite Ford into her bedroom. And the way she was feeling right now, a little lightheaded and totally enamored, that wouldn't be a good idea. "Tell you what. You go back to the hotel and change, and we'll meet back up for dinner."

"Okay. Just point me in the right direction."

"You can take the car. I'll write down how to get back to the hotel, and basically you just follow that route to get back here."

"Only one problem. I'm not authorized to drive your rental, and I don't have my license back yet."

"I trust you. Just don't run over any pedestrians along the way. Besides, it's not far at all. Just a few blocks."

"Are you sure?"

"Unless you can't drive anything other than a truck."

He released a low, deep laugh. "I can hold my own in a car."

Kerry just wished he was holding her. But tonight... Well, tonight she planned to have him hold her, and possibly more. She would play it by ear and see how things progressed between them. "Fine. Be back here at 7:00 p.m. You can meet my landlady then."

"Sounds good."

He looked good. No. He looked great, even drenched. Better than any man had a right to look, Kerry decided. She anticipated looking her fill later. "See you then."

Before she left the car, she leaned over and kissed his cheek. Yet when she pulled away, their gazes held for a long moment. That intangible chemistry came back to roost, and once more their lips came together in a fiery joining. They kissed for a long time, stopping only now and then to draw a breath. Kissed as if their very survival depended on it.

After a time, Ford cupped her jaw in his large palm, slid his hand down her throat. As ridiculous as it seemed, Kerry wanted him to keep going. She wanted him to touch her breasts, to know what that would be like to have that experience with a man that she wanted more than anything. A pleading sound escaped from her mouth and she guided his palm down to her breast, showing him what she needed. At the moment, she didn't really care what he might think of her, as long as he touched her. And he did, thoroughly, rubbing his thumb back and forth on her nipple until it formed a tight knot.

She shifted against the surge of heat between her thighs, wishing the console were gone and she could be closer to him.

Wishing for once that she'd been braver and invited him into the house. Wishing he would touch her beneath her shirt.

Ford broke the kiss and rested his lips against her ear as he continued to fondle her through the fabric. "We shouldn't be doing this."

Funny, Kerry was thinking exactly the opposite. "I know."

He kept his hand in motion despite his protest. "You're driving me crazy, Kerry."

"I could say the same thing about you."

All too soon, he took his hand away and collapsed back against the seat. "I've decided I'm not much better than that kid on the paddleboat."

Kerry tugged the band from her ponytail and finger-combed her hair. "Oh, I'm willing to wager you're much better than that kid. Experience is bound to count for something." She felt like a vamp, uninhibited and ready to take a few more chances.

Ford finally looked at her and groaned. "You are trying to kill me, aren't you?"

She frowned. "I don't know what you mean."

He reached over and sifted a lock through his fingertips. "You took your hair down. You look sexy as hell. And that's making things really *hard* on me."

She didn't dare look lower to confirm that fact. "Thank you."

"Wear it down tonight."

"I will. Any other requests?"

"Yeah. Be sure to wear a turtleneck and pants. Otherwise, I'm not going to responsible for my actions."

She laughed. "I'm probably going to nix the turtleneck, but I will be wearing some sort of a sweater. And you need to bring a jacket because the nights in San Francisco can be rather cool."

He leaned over the console, kissed her cheek, then whispered, "I'll keep you warm."

Kerry shivered at the thought, pleasantly so. "I'm looking forward to it."

After jotting down directions to the hotel on the back of the rental agreement, she grabbed the picnic basket from the backseat, opened the door and stepped outside while Ford did the same. They met in front of the hood, and before she could head toward the house, he pulled her back into his arms and she immediately dropped the basket onto the drive without a second thought. He kissed her again. This time their bodies completely melded together. She could feel every inch of him, from thighs to chest and everything in between. Definitely everything. Five more minutes and she *would* invite him into her bedroom, and quite possibly her bed.

The sound of a honking horn startled Kerry and sent her backward, away from Ford. She looked to her right to see Millie's ancient roadster waiting at the curb.

"That's Millie," Kerry said. "You'll have to back out before she can get up the drive."

"Not a problem." He gave her a crooked grin. "I probably need to get in the car anyway, before I totally lose my respectability."

This time Kerry did look. She just couldn't help herself. "I see." And she did.

"Yeah. I guess you do. But that's your fault."

She raised her gaze to his face. "Not all my fault, but I'm willing to take responsibility."

He took her hand, turned it over and kissed her palm. "I'm willing to compromise on the responsibility if you are."

"Oh, yes. I'm all about compromise." Right now she was all about being a mass of mercurial need.

After following Ford back to the driver's side, she leaned in and gave him another quick kiss before he closed the door. "I'll see you later. Call me if you get lost."

Lost was exactly how Kerry felt at the moment. Lost to a gorgeous Kansas farm boy. Lost to her own feminine urges for the very first time.

Now she had to decide exactly how far she would go to satisfy them.

# Four

Ford had no trouble finding his way back to Kerry. In fact, he'd spent the better part of an hour pacing with anticipation, and chastising himself for losing control again. Now he was sitting in the drive behind a gaudy ancient blue roadster, putting himself through the paces of a mental pep talk.

Tonight he would have dinner with her. He would slowly work his way into a conversation about Spencer's murder. He would keep his hands to himself.

That last directive was bugging the hell out of him because he wasn't sure he could follow through. Kerry Roarke was doing things to him no woman had done in a long time. He'd barely known her for twenty-four hours and already he was thinking things he should not be thinking. Considering things he should not be considering. He would just have to keep reminding himself of his mission, and remember that his uncle was wasting away in jail with a murder charge hanging over his head. And Ford could be the only person to save him from that fate—if Kerry cooperated.

He left the car and walked up the three steps, stopping to survey the grounds before knocking, as much out of procrastination as interest. The paint on the home's facade had begun to peel, and the flower beds had fallen into disarray. He also noticed that the porch's support seemed to be leaning and needed to be bolstered. Other than those few things, the estate still looked refined and shouted money.

After another brief hesitation, he rang the bell and jingled the keys in his pocket. He was still on edge, even more so when a severe-looking elderly woman opened the door. *Flamboyant* immediately came to Ford's mind, from her overly made-up face and jet-black hair to her flowing red-and-purple calf-length dress.

She eyed him curiously for a long moment before saying, "You must be Kerry's young man." She sounded polite but she didn't seem that pleased to see him.

"Yes, ma'am. Ford Matthews. And you must be Mrs. Vandiver." He stuck out his hand, which she took briefly for a delicate shake.

"You may call me Millie." She swept a hand in an almost theatrical gesture, her smile painted on as if also part of the act. "Right this way."

Ford stepped inside the foyer and followed behind her into a musty formal living room. She turned to him and said, "You may sit there," indicating an ancient gold sofa. While Ford settled onto the couch, Millie took a stiff-looking red chair across from him. The fabric was a near-match to the dress and her lips, contrasting with her pale skin. He couldn't quit peg her age, but from the looks of the myriad service awards lining the walls, many dating back decades, he'd guess she was somewhere around seventy.

Scooting to the edge of the chair, she studied him again. "Kerry tells me you're a farmer."

"Yes, I am."

"Do you make a decent living?"

If she only knew. "Yeah, I do all right."

She sat back, crossed one bony leg over the other and clasped her hands together in her lap. "Exactly what are your intentions, Ford?"

"I'm not sure I understand the question." He did understand he was about to get the third degree.

"What do you plan to do this evening with my charge?"

Her tone held a note of suspicion, like she'd channeled his questionable thoughts. "We're going out for dinner."

"And after that?"

"I'm not sure. We haven't discussed it."

She leaned forward and leveled her rheumy blue eyes on him. "May I speak frankly to you, Ford?"

Although she'd posed it as a question, Ford recognized he had no choice but to hear her out. Draping an arm over the back of the sofa, he tried to appear relaxed when he was any-thing but. "Sure."

"Kerry Ann is a very special young woman. She might ap-pear tough on the exterior, but that is only a front. Inside she is very vulnerable. Wounded, if you will."

Wounded? Ford's curiosity increased. "How do you mean?"

"It's not my place to say, but you must take my word for it. If she trusts you, she'll tell you. And if she does, then you should feel honored. Trust doesn't come easily for her, with good reason."

A good dose of guilt settled over Ford. "I understand."

"No, you don't. Not yet. But if you are lucky, you will. And one more thing."

"Shoot."

"I have protected her for many years, and I plan to continue to do so for as long as I am living. I will do anything, *anything,* to make certain she is not harmed. I suggest you keep that in mind. You certainly don't want to cross me." *And if you do, you won't live to tell about it,* her expression seemed to say.

One helluva scary woman, Ford decided. And it suddenly dawned on him that maybe this frail-looking lady could be a killer. Maybe she'd been the one to take out his grandfather in order to protect Kerry. A possibility, even if it was remote. Or maybe he just didn't want to believe that Kerry Roarke had been involved in Spencer's death. Only time would tell, if they ever got out of there so he could find out. "Do you think maybe Kerry's ready?"

She glanced at the clock set in the middle of a white marble mantel. "You are several minutes early." Again she nailed him with another severe glare. "I've always admired promptness, but then perhaps you are more eager than you should be."

Damn. Ford hadn't gotten this much cross examination since Grant had caught him playing with matches in the barn when he was ten years old. "I promise you I'll treat Kerry well."

"I am going to hold you to that promise, young man. That you can count on." Gripping the chair's arms, she pushed herself up slowly. "I shall go and see if she has completed her preparations."

"I'm here, Millie."

At the sound of Kerry's feather-soft voice coming from behind him, Ford realized he wasn't at all ready. He immediately came to his feet, turned and almost dropped where he stood when he caught sight of her standing in the entry wearing second-skin, low-riding jeans and a V-neck burgundy sweater than didn't quite meet her waistband, providing a glimpse of bare flesh at her belly. Falling to his knees would be a damned bad idea in front of the matriarch of the mansion.

Kerry slipped her purse strap over her slender shoulder. "Are you ready to roll, Ford?"

Oh, yeah, almost spilled out of his mouth before he had the presence of mind to stop it. "Sure. If you are."

"I am." After crossing the room, she planted a kiss on Millie's cheek. "Don't wait up, okay?"

Millie sent her a sour look. "I don't intend to do any such thing. You're a grown woman, Kerry Ann. I trust you." She stared at Ford, hard. "I trust you will take good care of her, young man?"

Ford had the sudden urge to salute. "Yes, ma'am. You can count on it."

"And I'm counting on you to do that very thing. Now, both of you, run along. Have a nice time."

But not too nice a time, Ford thought as he followed Kerry out the front door. Millie might not have said it, but her tone indicated she was thinking it. Sound advice all the way around.

Ford tossed Kerry the car key. "You drive around this maze of a city."

Kerry tossed him a sexy smile. "I plan to."

Five minutes in her presence and she was already driving him crazy. He bordered on crossing over into complete madness when they settled into the car and her perfume hit him full force. She smelled like a hint of flowers mixed with fruit, something he might normally consider an odd combination, but not on her. He imagined she tasted as good, too. All over.

Twitching in his seat, he snapped his seat belt closed while Kerry lowered the roof on the car now that the threat of rain had subsided. The sun was on the verge of setting while Ford was on the verge of kissing her. He decided that was the last thing he needed to do and promised himself to refrain for now.

At least this time, Kerry didn't make a move to kiss him,

either. Instead, she started the car, put it in gear and backed out of the steep drive like a pro. "I hope Millie didn't give you a hard time," she said as she turned onto the street.

"Not too bad. I'm not sure she likes me."

"Millie likes everyone. She's just cautious."

"I kind of figured that out."

She sent him a glance as they stopped at a light. "What did she say to you exactly?"

"Just that I needed to be careful with you."

"She's very protective of me."

"I gathered that right away. Hopefully I put her mind at ease."

She rolled through the light and turned sharply onto a major street. "Don't worry about Millie. The important thing is that I know you're not going to hurt me."

God, he didn't want to hurt her, but he realized he could. Especially if this whole theory about her being Spencer's mistress was in error. "So where are you taking me tonight?"

"To one of my favorite restaurants in one of my favorite places. It's in an area known as The Haight."

Hippie haven, that's how Ford had termed Kerry's old stomping grounds. In many ways that was still true, she realized. But the place had transformed from a flower-child hangout to a trendy hotspot with shops and restaurants, although it still retained a lot of its sixties roots. Kerry knew the back alleys and communal existence very well. She'd spent a lot of days in those places upon her arrival in San Francisco. She'd learned quite a bit about hard living during that time in her life, some of which she still carried with her—on her body and in her soul.

She wanted to tell Ford about that part of her past, minus the really horrible part, but she experienced the burden of being labeled "homeless" and not knowing how people would react to that. Whenever she'd chosen to be honest with her co-workers, some had been accepting and sympathetic, others had been judgmental and treated her as damaged goods. Some saw her as an as easy mark, and that had included Spencer Ashton.

She decided not to contaminate the conversation right now. Dinner had gone so well that she wanted to keep the mood light. Ford had been very pleased that she'd taken him to a place where he could dine on a burger and fries. She had been pleased to have pleased him. But now that dinner was over, she had to decide what would happen next. If she went according to plan, a drive to another special place would be first on the agenda. What happened after that would be up to Ford.

Ford insisted on paying the bill again and that bothered her somewhat. She wasn't broke even though finances were tight. Real estate courses had drained most of her savings but she planned to eventually get ahead as soon as she'd completed the program in two weeks. Then she could quit her current job after she obtained her license and signed on as an agent, concentrating on her dream—finding families permanent homes, something she hadn't really had, aside from her home with Millie. But it still hadn't been the same, because it wasn't hers. One day, she would have a home of her own, and maybe even someone to share it with.

She glanced at Ford and wished that he could be the man of her dreams. Unfortunately, that wasn't reality. Soon he would be leaving, but she refused to think about that now. She planned to make the best of their time together and hopefully restore herself into the land of the living under his guidance. If he happened to be willing. She would just have to convince him that's what she wanted. No strings attached, just memories to make.

Kerry and Ford left the restaurant and strolled up the sidewalk toward the pay-by-the-hour parking lot. Along the way she pointed out the surfer shop with several colorful boards on display in the window. "This might interest you," she said, followed by a laugh.

He frowned. "Why would you think that? I've never even tried surfing. Not many beaches near where I live."

She paused and faced him. "Because when I first saw you in the bar, I thought you looked like a surfer with that blond hair and tanned body. Or is that just a farmer's tan you have?"

His grin gave the streetlight some serious competition. "Are you asking me if I'm tanned all over?"

"Yes, I guess that's what I'm asking."

"Do you want to see?"

Frankly, she did. "It's a little cool to be taking off your shirt." But not cool enough to rid Kerry of some serious heat prompted by that thought.

"You're right, but if you decide you want proof, all you have to do is ask."

She just might ask before the night was over. "Okay, I will. Now let's get back to the car. I have another place I want to show you."

"Okay. You're the boss."

Taking Kerry by surprise, Ford leaned over and kissed her cheek. A simple gesture, but one that touched her in complex ways. "What was that for?"

"For being such a great tour guide. I owe you a lot."

"This whole experience with you has been a pleasure." More pleasure than she'd expected. Hopefully more pleasure to come. "But it's not over yet, unless you're tired and want to go to bed." She regretted the comment that came out sounding like suggestive innuendo. "I meant to sleep."

Ford's provocative smile came into play slowly. "I don't want to sleep. In fact, I'm not tired at all."

"Good." She hooked her arm into the bend of his arm. "Then let's get on with the second phase of the evening."

By the time they made the block, they had their arms wrapped securely around each other's waists, as if they were any other couple out on a date. Kerry felt completely comfortable with this man, totally relaxed, a huge step in the right direction. She couldn't say the same for Ford when he tensed as they came upon a lanky teenage boy with tattered clothes, listless eyes and his hand out.

"Could you spare a few bucks?" the teen said, his voice tentative and almost apologetic.

Suddenly thrust back in time, Kerry did the only thing she could do. She released her hold on Ford's arm and dug through her purse for a ten-dollar bill and a card. She held both up before handing them over. "I'll give you this as long as you promise me no drugs. What's your name?"

"Joe." The boy's gaze faltered. "No drugs. I just want something to eat."

"I understand, Joe." Kerry handed over the money and the card. "You'll find the address for a shelter where you can get a bath and clean clothes. Tell Rosie I sent you. She might even be able to find you a job. How old are you?"

"Seventeen."

Kerry wondered if he was lying about his age because he didn't look a day over fifteen, if that. "Good luck, Joe. And get some help. The streets are no place to be, even for a guy."

Finally he smiled. A small one, but a smile all the same. "Thanks. I'll try."

Ford had stood by silently during the exchange. He remained quiet all the way back to the car and during the drive across the Golden Gate Bridge and up into the hills that comprised the Marin Headlands. Kerry accepted that silence for now, yet knowing the time would come when she would have to offer an explanation, because she knew he would eventually ask.

After she parked in the pull-off spot that offered a spectacular view of the city, Kerry left the car and Ford followed her lead. She opened the trunk and retrieved two blankets, a thick one to cover the ground, the other to shelter them against the chilly night air. Kerry was definitely chilled, but only in part from the weather. Ford's continued coolness toward her made her nervous and fearful that once he knew the details of her past, their evening together could come to an abrupt halt. She didn't want it to end, not yet.

Ford had turned his back on her to stare at the amazing panorama—the outline of the bridge, the water shimmering beneath the three-quarter moon and the city lights twinkling in the distance. Or maybe he was simply avoiding her.

No longer able to stand his silence, she moved to a spot not far away from him on the edge leading to the cliffs. With one hand, she spread the thicker blanket over the grass as best she could and kept the other clutched against her chest. "The view's breathtaking, isn't it?" she said as she studied his strong profile and his lips that formed a tight line.

"Yeah, it is." He still had yet to look at her.

Kerry lowered herself onto the blanketed ground, hoping upon hope he would join her. "It's a lot more comfortable down here."

He turned toward her, his thumbs hooked in the pockets of his black leather jacket. Even in the muted light, he was an imposing, beautiful presence silhouetted against the night sky.

Kerry released the breath she'd been holding when he took his place beside her, yet not quite as close as she would have liked. He rested his forearms on his bent knees, his hands laced together. She sensed he wanted to speak, and he confirmed that by saying, "You handled that kid well. I'm not sure

I would've given him money, though. Especially if he might spend it on drugs."

"He needed some kind of a break, probably even more than the money. I just hope he finds a safe place to land, at least for the night."

Ford sent her a brief glance before he turned his attention back to the scenery. "How did you know about the homeless shelter?"

Exactly what she'd been expecting, and dreading. "I've volunteered there before." Only a partial truth. Once upon a terrible time, she'd temporarily resided there.

"I don't understand why a kid would want to live on the streets."

Kerry reached down and pulled the other blanket over her as if it might provide some protection from his possible reaction. "I'm sure he doesn't want to live this way. He's probably a runaway."

"Running away isn't the answer."

Sometimes it was the only answer. "Try telling that to a teenager who honestly believes he or she doesn't have a choice."

Finally he looked at her straight-on. "I have a hard time believing that things would be so bad at home that someone feels escaping is the only option."

"Believe me, it can be that bad. So bad that you don't think there is another way. You feel so trapped you can't see beyond getting out."

When she saw unease in his expression, Kerry realized she had revealed too much. He confirmed that by saying, "You sound like you know all about it."

Now was the time to tell him the truth and accept his response, whatever that response might be. "I do know because I ran away. And for one solid year, I was homeless."

She saw momentary shock in his expression and possibly sympathy. "How old were you?"

"Sixteen."

"So young and on your own?"

"Yeah. I came to a point where I thought I had no choice but to leave. My stepfather was cruel and verbally abusive. My mother never seemed to notice it when she was alive, or maybe she didn't want to see it. Then one day I stood up to him and he backhanded me across the face. I honestly thought he might try to kill me. Later that night, I packed a bag, stole a hundred dollars from his wallet and caught a bus for San Francisco."

"And he never came looking for you?"

Kerry released a mirthless laugh. "I doubt it. Many times he told me he ought to kick me out. I was worthless and a burden. Funny thing, I was a straight-A student, never in trouble, but I couldn't seem to do anything to please him. I stopped trying."

"I'm sorry," he said, and he sounded that way, as well.

"It's not your fault. Besides, I met Millie a year later, and she was the best thing that ever happened to me."

"How exactly did you meet her?"

That circumstance was getting into territory Kerry wasn't sure she was ready to cover. She decided to settle on a condensed version. "One night I got into a fight and ended up in the hospital with a few scrapes and bruises. A nurse in the E.R. knew Millie liked to help runaways, so she called her. Millie took me in that night, and I ended up staying. She home-schooled me because we didn't want the hassle of having to explain guardianship, and then I eventually got my G.E.D. I also went to community college and majored in business. Unfortunately, I only received an associate's degree so my job options were limited. That's why I've been attending real estate school in the evenings."

He studied her for a time before saying, "I admire you, Kerry. I don't know how you survived on your own at that age."

"That experience made me much tougher," she said. "Survival is the name of the game, and living alone on the streets taught me that." It had also taught her caution, and a definite lack of trust, especially in men. Spencer Ashton had only cemented that mistrust. But Ford Matthews was different, that's what her instincts were telling her. She felt as if she could sincerely trust both them and him.

"At least you did get a decent job," Ford said after a time.

Some job. "Unfortunately, working for an indecent lecher."

"Lecher?"

"That sums up Spencer Ashton in a nutshell."

"What did he do to you?" He looked and sounded angry.

Kerry plucked at a blade of grass and shredded it. "Aside from pawing me, he used to stage these little lunches under the guise of business meetings. Some were even out of the city. When I wouldn't *cooperate,* he buried me in work and refused to give me a raise. I honestly think he believed I would finally give in."

"There are laws against sexual harassment. Why didn't you report him or at least quit?"

"First of all, I needed the money. Second, Spencer Ashton had a lot of power and connections. Even after his death he's still revered as a city leader." She sighed. "And God forgive me for saying this, I understand why someone would want him dead. But I think they might have arrested the wrong person."

Ford leveled a hard stare on her. "Why do you think that?"

"I just do." She couldn't imagine a man as polite as Grant Ashton would be a killer. For months he'd tried to get in to see his father, his anger never directed at her when she'd refused to allow him access, per Spencer's instructions. But Spencer had been known for his charm, so she could be wrong about his son. After all, he was an Ashton, and that name alone made her cringe.

Ford draped his arm around her shoulder and pulled her close to his side. "After hearing about this bastard, I agree with you. I don't think anyone would have blamed anyone for getting even."

Kerry reveled in his warmth, in his compassion. "Oh, I did get even in my own way." Ways she was too embarrassed to tell him. Nothing major enough to risk ending up in the unemployment line, but a few childish things to give her some measure of satisfaction. Proof positive that you could take the girl off the streets, but you couldn't take the street out of the girl.

Ford surveyed her face from forehead to chin, his expression sympathetic, not cynical. "I'm sorry for what you've had to endure, with both your situation at home and with your boss."

"Again, it's not your fault." She reached up and formed her palm to his shadowed jaw. "I've learned to tolerate what life throws me, Ford. I've had to. But I've also learned not to dwell on the past. You just have to move on, otherwise you find yourself too afraid to go forward." And that hit home right then more than any other time in her life. Tonight she refused to be afraid. She only wanted to experience true freedom from fear, and she knew that Ford Matthews could be the man to help her over that fear.

On that thought, she brushed a kiss over his cheek, then one along his jaw, making her way to the corner of his mouth and stopping there. A subtle suggestion, but it worked. He inclined his head and kissed her, carefully at first, until care gave way to carnal.

After pulling the quilt from her shoulders and tossing it aside, Kerry took Ford with her back onto the remaining blanket without disrupting the kiss. She kept her arms tightly around him while his hands roved down her sides. She wanted so much more, enough to break the kiss and tug the sweater over her head. While he watched, with one hand she reached up to unfasten the bra's front closure, with the other she guided his palm to her breast. He touched her with innate gentleness, working her nipple between his fingertips for a time before replacing his hand with his mouth.

Kerry tuned in to every sensation, every light flick of his tongue across her nipple, every gentle pull of his lips as she stared up at the misty sky, her hands buried in his thick hair. The infamous San Francisco fog had begun to appear above them in swirls, giving the moon a muted, dreamlike glow. Everything about this night had taken on a surreal quality, but the overwhelming need she now experienced was extremely real.

Ford lifted his head from her breast and stared at her a long moment. "You are so damn beautiful."

Kerry truly felt beautiful when she noted the approval in his eyes, but that soon turned to concern when he traced a fingertip along the scar spanning from her rib cage to beneath her left breast. "What happened here?"

She'd tried to defend herself and lost. Lost what little had remained of her sense of security, and her innocence. "I'd rather not talk about that now." Doing so would only resurrect more bitter memories. Tonight she only wanted to make more memories. Good ones.

After shoving the leather jacket from Ford's broad shoulders, Kerry worked it off his arms and tossed it aside. Then she pulled the tails of his shirt from his jeans, released the buttons and opened it wide to smooth her hands over his chest.

Although he looked somewhat troubled, she also saw a definite fire in his blue eyes. "Kerry, if we don't stop now, I might not be able to stop."

"I don't want you to stop." She locked into his gaze. "I

don't need any promises. I only need you to touch me again. Everywhere."

As if his last shred of control had snapped, Ford pulled her to face him, molding his hands to her scalp, holding her in place to accept the provocative play of his tongue against hers. After rolling her onto her back, he moved partially atop her and she could feel his erection pressing against her pelvis. Could feel his heart pounding against her breast where their bodies met without any barriers between them.

Kerry wanted all the barriers gone. She wanted to know how it would feel to have him totally naked against her, inside her. She wanted to know all of him and in turn, learn how it felt to truly make love with a man without reservation or coercion.

He broke the kiss and once more rolled her to face him, settling her head against his shoulder, his warm breath breezing over her ear as he let go a mild oath in a harsh whisper. She celebrated her sudden sense of power. Rejoiced in the fact that she could take him so close to the edge. Only, she was following right behind him.

As Ford claimed her mouth in another tantalizing kiss, he parted her legs with his leg and rubbed against the apex of her thighs. The friction the denim created was both delicious and frustrating. She *needed* him to touch her without any clothing constraints. Emboldened by her own newly discovered empowerment, she took his hand from the bow of her hip and placed it on her abdomen where her low-riding jeans began below her navel. She hoped he would take the hint, take the initiative to make her wish come true. She feared she wouldn't get that wish when he pulled his leg from between hers. But when she felt the tug on the jeans' button, then the slide of her zipper, her optimism rose and so did her heart rate.

He kept one hand tangled in her hair and slid his other palm beneath the backside of her jeans, kneading her bottom through her panties. For Kerry, it wasn't quite enough so she pushed against him, letting him know exactly where she needed his attention though he probably did know. In order to be assured, she reached between them and tugged on his fly, only to have Ford catch her wrist before she had it undone.

Confused, she looked at him straight-on and saw indecision warring in his eyes, and something else she couldn't quite identify. "What's wrong?" she asked, her voice as shaky as her body.

Everything, Ford thought. As badly as he wanted to finish this, he didn't dare. As badly as he wanted to lose himself deep inside her, he couldn't do it. Not without losing what was left of his honor.

After tossing the discarded blanket over Kerry to cover her, he sat up, draped his forearms on his bent knees and lowered his eyes to the blanket beneath him.

Kerry's hand coming to rest on his shoulder was almost his undoing. "If you're worried about safety, I've taken care of that."

Ford glanced over his shoulder to see her holding a condom that he assumed had been in her pocket. She'd had all the bases covered, and protection hadn't even crossed his mind. That's how far gone he'd been. He didn't know how he had let things get so out of control. Easy. His head had been screwed up the moment he'd laid eyes on her. God help him, he had totally lost his mind, and had damn near lost his principles. Disregarded everything his uncle had taught him about respecting women. Behaved no better than his bastard of a grandfather.

"I'm not like him," he muttered without thought.

"Like who?"

"Spencer Ashton."

"I know you're not like him."

But he would be if he continued on this course. Right now he had something he had to ask her, before he revealed the truth. But he wasn't quite ready to face her, so he kept his back turned. "I need to know something, Kerry."

"If you want to know if I've been with a man, yes. But only one. And not by choice."

*Not by choice.* "You were…?" He couldn't even force himself to say the ugly word.

"Raped. For a long time I had a hard time saying it, too. But with the help of counselors and support groups and Millie, and even helping others, I've come a long way. It's something you don't ever forget, but you move on and get stronger as the years go by. At least I have. "

Ford's concerns increased and he had to ask, even if he feared the answer. "Was it Spencer Ashton?"

"No. It happened a long time ago, the night I went to live with Millie."

While she was still fending for herself on the streets, he realized. At the age of sixteen. He was only slightly relieved that his own flesh and blood hadn't physically assaulted her even though he'd terrorized her in many ways. He honestly wished he knew who had attacked her because right now he wouldn't think twice about killing him with his bare hands. He'd almost done that very thing to the jerk who'd tried to assault Abby years ago. Still, he'd known for years how much that event had affected Abby, even if she had rammed her knee into a strategic area before it had been too late, saving herself from Kerry's fate.

Ford shifted around to face Kerry again, thankful to find that she was completely dressed, her legs crossed before her, her hands fisted on her thighs. "I wish you would have told me sooner."

She hugged her arms to her breasts. "Would that have

made a difference? I mean, you stopped anyway." She inclined her head and stared at him. "Why did you stop?"

Now for the most difficult question of all, the entire reason why he'd met her in the first place. "I have to know something, Kerry. Did you have anything to do with Spencer Ashton's murder?"

Her eyes went wide. "Why would you even think that?"

"Because you said they've arrested the wrong man. That you found a way to get even with him. And considering what you've been through, I couldn't blame you if you did."

She let go a humorless laugh. "I got *even* as in I put salt in his coffee and scheduled his least favorite clients back-to-back. And for your information, I was at my real estate classes in the Bay area the night he was killed. I didn't even know about it until I came in the next morning." Awareness mixed with anger reflected from her face. "That's why you stopped, because you think I'm a murderer?"

He'd stopped because she had no idea who he was, but before he could spit it out, she uncrossed her legs and came to her knees, leaving very little space between them. "Let me tell you something, Ford. I watched a man die once, and he wasn't considered a good man. In fact, he was a drug dealer. Someone shot him only a few feet away from where I was hanging out. I'll never forget it. And even though I knew he destroyed lives, I also knew that no one had the right to take his life. Believe me, I could never kill anyone, even if I did hate them with a passion."

The sincerity in her expression confirmed what Ford had probably known all along—she hadn't been involved in any way in Spencer's death. She hadn't been his mistress, either. "I do believe you. And I'm sorry I doubted you."

She laid a palm on his arm. "Then can we stop talking and go back to where we were a few moments before?"

After he said what he needed to say, she would probably prefer he go back to Nebraska. "I sure as hell wish we could, but we can't."

She dropped her hand and released her frustration on a sigh. "Why not?"

"Because you don't know me. You don't know—"

She pressed a fingertip to his lips. "I know all that I need to know. I know you're a good man. I know that you've accepted what I've told you about my past without judgment. I also know that I trust you enough to make love with you. It's taken me a long time to be willing to take that step, and I want to do that with you."

She might as well have delivered a two-fisted punch to his gut. "You shouldn't trust me, Kerry, because I've been lying to you."

Her whole frame went rigid. "You're married."

"No, I'm not married. But I'm from Nebraska, not Kansas." The time had come for Ford to lay it on the line. He was more than willing to accept the consequences and her fury. He deserved that much and more. "I'm Spencer Ashton's grandson."

# Five

The exhilaration Kerry had experienced only a few short moments ago disappeared like the moonlight now obscured by the fog. She clutched the blanket to her chest as if it provided security as well as cover. "I don't understand," she said, although she feared she did.

"My name is Ford Ashton, not Ford Matthews. Grant is my uncle. He raised me. I came to California to try and find out anything I can to clear him."

The bitter truth came with a stinging bite of betrayal. "Are you telling me that our meeting—"

"Wasn't an accident. I thought you might have information."

"You thought I murdered him." Her voice held an edge of disbelief, exactly what she was feeling at the moment. Disbelief and so many more emotions crowding in on her all at once.

He lowered his gaze once more. "I was told you might be involved because you were Spencer's mistress."

"Whoever told you that was dead wrong. I hated the man."

"I know that now."

She released a caustic laugh. "This is so rich. You seduced me for the sake of information. I think I would've preferred to be held at knife point."

Finally he looked at her, remorse in his eyes. Probably just another lie, Kerry decided. "I never intended for this to happen," he said. "You have to believe that, even if you don't believe anything else."

"Believe you? Why should I believe anything you say when everything you've told me has been a lie?"

"Not everything. I do want you, more than I've wanted any woman I can think of. And I care about you, that's why this is so damn difficult. I didn't plan on that, either."

Kerry came to her feet and turned her back to Ford, refastened her bra then pulled the sweater over her head. She then grabbed up the discarded blanket with shaking hands without looking at him. She didn't want to see his eyes that she'd thought had been honest. See his hands that had touched her so thoroughly and gently.

All lies. What a fool she'd been to trust him. What a stupid, stupid fool.

He moved in front of her, the remaining blanket bunched in his strong arms. "I want to talk about this some more. I want to try to explain."

No explanation would be good enough, as far as Kerry was concerned. "I have a good mind to make you walk back into the city. But I'm more benevolent than that, although I'm not sure why."

He streaked a hand over the back of his neck. "I'm sorry. I don't know what else to say."

She wanted him to say this was all a bad dream. That what they had shared was as pure and true as it had seemed. "I don't care to hear anything else you have to say. I'm going to take you back to the hotel, and then I'm going to put you and this whole experience out of my mind." Probably not an easy feat because no matter how much he'd betrayed her, she would never forget him, or the feelings for him that had begun to creep into her heart and soul. Feelings for the man she'd thought him to be.

Without another word, Kerry turned away from Ford, headed back to the Mustang and tossed the blanket into the backseat while he did the same from the passenger side. Once they were in the car, she took off in a rush, not bothering to put up the top on the convertible, leaving behind what she'd thought would be good memories in the dust.

As they drove, the wind bit into her cheeks and numbed her face but unfortunately did nothing to numb the ache in her heart. She tuned the radio to a jazz station and turned the volume high, trying to drown out all the questions running through her mind, without success. Ford didn't speak at all, didn't even look at her, and she tried not to look at him although at times her eyes betrayed her. When they stopped at the booth on the bridge, he reached across her to hand the attendant the toll, his arm brushing slightly across her breast. She didn't want to react to that, didn't want to remember, but she did.

They continued on in silence as they entered the city and made their way up the hill, first to his hotel where she would leave him behind and then go home, where she might have a good cry. Once she reached the portico in front of the Royal-brook, she stopped the car alongside the curb but didn't bother to put it in Park. "Good night," she told him, followed by, "and good luck," muttering the words with little enthusiasm.

A few moments ticked off and still he didn't leave. She could feel his gaze on her and sensed he wanted to speak. She doubted he had anything to say that she wanted to hear.

"I'm sorry, Kerry."

Territory they'd already covered, and Kerry still had a hard time believing it. "Fine. You're sorry. Great."

"I hate what I've done to you. I hate myself for feeling like I had to do it. I was so damn desperate to get Grant cleared that I would've done anything to see that happen. That's my only excuse."

Admittedly, she knew all about desperation, but that didn't excuse him in her mind. "Desperate enough to lie to someone you didn't even know, and to assume the worst about her?"

"I'm not proud of it." He reached over and set the gear into Park. "But that much is the truth. Desperation drives people to do things they wouldn't normally do."

She shifted to face him and draped one arm over the steering wheel. "All you had to do was tell me the truth. I would have answered your questions."

"Would you if you'd known I'm an Ashton?"

Probably not, Kerry decided. "I guess we'll never know, will we?"

He rubbed a hand over his jaw. "I just want you to know that I've never done anything like this before."

And she had never done with any man what she had done with him. "What, pretend you're someone you're not? Or pretend you want someone in order to get what you need?"

"You're an incredible woman, Kerry. When I said I wanted you, it wasn't a lie." He reached over and brushed a strand of hair away from her face. "I still do, and that's the honest-to-God truth."

With that, he left the car and strode into the hotel. Kerry watched him until she could no longer see him, then with heavy limbs and an even heavier heart, she drove away. Drove home in a mental haze, thankful the streets weren't all that crowded due to the lateness of the hour.

By the time she walked through the front door, all she wanted was a hot bath and her bed. What she got was Millie sitting regally in her favorite chair, looking expectant. "Did you have a good time, dearest?"

What a joke. "I thought I told you not to wait up." She hadn't meant to sound so cross but she couldn't seem to control her emotions.

"What's happened, Kerry Ann?" Millie kept her tone even, but it didn't mask the concern in her eyes.

Kerry collapsed onto the sofa and tossed her purse aside. "Nothing happened, other than he lied to me."

"Lied about what?"

She didn't really have the energy to rehash the evening, but she knew Millie wouldn't let up until she came clean. "As it turns out, Ford Matthews is really Ford Ashton, the grandson of my deceased boss and the nephew of the man arrested for the murder. He was wooing me in order to find out if I knew anything about Spencer Ashton's death in order to clear his uncle."

"Why would he think you would know anything?"

"Someone told him I was Spencer's mistress, if you can imagine that. The man was a bastard and an egomaniac who saw every one of his assistants as an easy target. I had absolutely no use for him. But I didn't have him murdered, although a few times I did consider knocking him over the head with a paperweight when he tried to grab my butt."

Millie frowned. "Why didn't you tell me this sooner? I know many of the Ashton-Lattimer board members. I could have stopped the man's harassment."

Kerry doubted that, in light of Spencer's standing with the company, governing board or no governing board. "I needed to handle it myself, Millie. I can't keep relying on you to rescue me."

"And this Ford believed you had Spencer killed?"

"He thought it was a possibility, but now he knows he was wrong. At least, I think he does. I'm not sure what to believe anymore."

With narrowed eyes, Millie studied Kerry's face. "Did he do anything inappropriate to you?"

Nothing she hadn't wanted. "Actually, I practically threw myself at him because I thought I could trust him. He stopped before things went too far. He said he couldn't lie to me any longer and then he told me who he is. End of story."

Millie tented her hands beneath her chin. "I must admit, my opinion of him has risen."

That almost shocked the life out of Kerry. "You're defending him?"

"You said he's trying to clear his uncle?"

"Yes. The man who raised him."

"And he would do anything to do that, I take it."

"Yes, and that included lying to me even before he had all the facts."

"But when the opportunity presented itself to have his way with you, he stopped."

Kerry's gaze drifted away from Millie's steady gaze. "Yes."

"My dear, it takes a very strong man to pass up such an opportunity since the majority of the male species is ruled by baser urges. It also takes a man with a strong sense of honor."

Kerry had to admit the truth in Millie's assertions even if she wanted to deny them. "I realize that, but he had other opportunities to tell me earlier."

"I assume this is true, but he was on a mission to protect someone he loves. I can understand that. I would do anything to protect you, my angel."

How well Kerry knew that. She also knew Millie meant serious business when she joined her on the sofa. "Kerry Ann,

I sense that you have feelings for this man, despite what he's done to you. Did he express any true remorse?"

"He tried. He said he was sorry he hurt me. He said he cared about me." That he wanted her. That she was an incredible woman. "He also said he had only one excuse for his behavior, desperation."

"And he saw you as his only hope to help his uncle. Perhaps you are still his only hope."

Kerry's mouth dropped open before she snapped it shut. "What are you saying?"

"I'm saying perhaps you should put your anger aside and help him. The good you do for another will come back to you tenfold in blessings."

"I don't know what I could do to help him. I told the police everything I know about the circumstances leading to the murder."

"I'm not referring to the murder. Your young man could use a friend, a 'leaning shoulder,' so to speak. You can offer your support and friendship if you cannot offer anything else. One never knows what might result from an act of kindness, and the true power of forgiveness."

Kerry mulled that over for a few moments while Millie continued to scrutinize her. Could she go back to Ford Ashton and forgive him? Could she simply be there for him as a friend, knowing that in a secret place in her soul, she wanted more? And would she be trading her heart in exchange?

She was a scrapper. She'd survived the streets. She's survived Spencer. She could take on Ford Ashton without losing herself totally to a man who had nothing to offer. Or could she?

"Okay, Millie, I'll think about what you've said. And tomorrow I'll decide if I can be his friend. But only his friend."

Millie's eyes held a world of wisdom. "Yes, my angel, you can be his friend. You might even be his savior."

* * *

Ford had spent most of Sunday dragging around from lack of sleep, scraping his mind for what to do next and missing a woman he had no business missing.

After returning a call from Caroline, who'd informed him he had an appointment with the attorney in the morning, he'd taken a shower and decided to settle in for the evening on the sofa, not bothering to put on any clothes. He considered watching baseball, but that didn't seem all that interesting. The selection of movies on pay-per-view didn't, either. He sure as hell didn't dare tune in to the adult offerings, considering what had transpired with Kerry last night. Their confrontation had effectively shut off his libido, but that had been only temporary. In fact, unanswered need had kept him up most of the night. So had self-hatred over what he'd done to her, especially now that he knew the horror of her past. But he still wanted her, more than he could express. Truth was, he couldn't have her. Not now. Not ever.

When a series of knocks sounded at the door, Ford pushed off the sofa and grabbed his jeans from the nearby chair, hopping on one foot to shrug them on while calling, "Just a minute."

He didn't have a clue who would be visiting him so late in the evening, but he hoped it wasn't any of the Ashton clan. He was shirtless, unshaven, sleep-deprived and sexually keyed up. Not a good combination to greet his newly discovered family members.

Ford opened the door to discover the subject of his daydreams standing on the other side of threshold, her hair curling slightly over her breasts encased in a form-fitting, off-the-shoulder green top, her long legs exposed by a matching skirt that hit her mid thigh. He was so damned shocked to see her that he almost closed the door then opened it again, just to make sure his imagination hadn't distorted his vision.

She hugged her arms to her middle. "May I come in?"

Like she really had to ask. "Sure." Ford stepped aside, and she breezed by him. She smelled great, his first thought. She looked even better, his second.

After he closed the door behind him, Ford turned to see her standing in the middle of the sitting area, her purse clutched to her chest. He couldn't quite read her expression, or even guess why she was there. Probably to give him a good tongue lashing, and not the preferred kind.

"Nice suite," she said after surveying the room. "A good view of the city."

The best view was standing right in front of him. "Why are you here, Kerry?"

"I've been thinking about what you said last night," she began. "And I've decided to help you."

Ford hadn't expected that for a minute. But then, she hadn't met his expectations on several levels. She wasn't mistress material. She wasn't a murderer. She was kind and unselfish and forgiving, everything a man could ask for in a woman. Yet he knew that anything beyond a continuing friendship with her would never happen now, and he deserved that. He didn't deserve her compassion, but here she was offering it in spite of his lies.

"Let's sit down," she said, and took the lone chair, leaving the sofa as Ford's only option.

He dropped down onto the cushions, fighting the urge to climb across the coffee table now separating them and kiss her. "How are you going to help me?"

"I've decided I'm going to be your friend, because you're probably going to need one until you get this thing with your uncle settled, one way or the other."

He needed her in ways he hadn't imagined, and it didn't have only to do with sex. "What made you change your mind?"

She moved slightly and looked away. "Because I know what it's like to be up against insurmountable odds and not have anyone to rely on."

In other words, odds were he probably wouldn't find the evidence needed to clear Grant. Nor would he ever be able to hold her again. To kiss her again, although God knew he wanted that. "I appreciate your offer."

She turned her gaze on him. "You sound disappointed."

He was disappointed, but not in the way that she thought. "No, I'm grateful. I'm just beat." But not tired enough to consider taking up where they left off last night.

Kerry quickly came to her feet. "Then I'll let you go to bed."

Going to bed didn't interest him, unless she went with him. "I probably couldn't sleep anyway. Please sit back down."

"I have to be at work in the morning."

He stood. "It's still early." He sounded almost desperate to keep her there. Maybe he was. "You don't have to stay that long."

"Okay. For a while." She dropped her purse at her feet and reclaimed her seat in the chair as Ford collapsed back on the couch.

She studied him a long moment with concern. "Have you had anything decent to eat today?"

Come to think of it, he hadn't, not anything of real substance. Just a few minibar pretzels to go with the shot of whiskey he'd had earlier that afternoon. "Not really."

She leaned forward, grabbed up the room service menu from the coffee table and pored over it. "They have a good selection of beef. I hear the prime rib is good."

"Do you want anything?"

She kept flipping through the menu before wetting her lips, drawing Ford's undivided attention. "I've already had dinner, but I wouldn't mind some dessert. Maybe a chocolate sundae."

What Ford wanted for dessert had nothing to do with ice cream. "Not a problem." Taking a chance, he stood and crossed the room to stand behind the sofa, peering over her shoulder, all too aware that the need to touch her was stronger than his need for food. "Turn back to the entrées."

She looked up at him as if she had no idea what an entrée was. When she didn't respond, Ford leaned down and flipped through the menu, their arms brushing. Even the limited contact did things to Ford that he needed to avoid for the sake of his sanity. He stopped at the all-day dining section and pointed. "I'm going to have the roast beef sandwich."

"Is that enough for you?"

Just having her there would be enough. For now. "Yeah."

"Fine." She slapped the menu closed and handed it to him. "I'd like a slice of cheesecake, strawberry topping. And some coffee."

"Great. I'll call it in."

Ford walked to the desk, tossed down the menu and dialed room service without looking back at her. If he contacted those violet eyes, he wouldn't be able to form a coherent sentence. He couldn't quite explain why she continued to affect him so strongly. Again, he could continue to chalk it up to lust, or admit to himself it went deeper than that. He could handle simple desire. Deeper he couldn't deal with. But he'd have to deal with it or lose his connection with her. He didn't want to face that again, at least until the time came for him to go back home.

After he placed the order, Ford turned to find Kerry had taken a seat on one end of the sofa. Progress, he thought, but decided it best not to act on any of his considerations of what he'd like to do to her. Otherwise he'd be pushing his luck and, in turn, pushing her right out the door. He strode to the sofa and immediately noticed she was sizing him up—and down. And up again. When he sat, leaving only a small space between them, she smiled. He'd give up food for days just to see that smile, that single dimple creasing the corner of her mouth. A really great spot to kiss.

"What?" he asked when she continued to grin.

"I just noticed you do have a tan all over. Or at least on your chest."

"You didn't notice that last night?"

"It was dark last night, and you didn't take your shirt off completely."

Thinking back on the events of last night had big trouble threatening below his belt. He hooked a thumb over his shoulder in the direction of the bedroom. "Maybe I should put one on now."

"Don't do that on my account. You might as well be comfortable."

He wouldn't be at all comfortable in her presence, considering how badly he wanted to touch her again and knowing that wasn't possible. "As long as it doesn't bother you."

"It doesn't. But I am curious about your tan. Maybe you *are* actually a surfer."

"I told you last night I've never surfed." One of the few truths he'd told her. "I sometimes ride the tractor without my shirt. My sister gives me hell about it even though I've told her it's cooler. She claims that wearing a shirt keeps the heat away." And little did Abby know, he'd spent more than a few afternoon breaks lying on the lounge chair poolside at his house, buck naked.

"You know, your sister is right," Kerry said after a thoughtful pause.

"If you ask her, she'll tell you she's always right. Stubborn woman."

"Do you have any other siblings?"

"Just Abby. We're a little less than two years apart."

"I take it you're close."

"Yeah, we've always been close." Bound together by their mother's abandonment and the mystery of their biological fathers. "Lately she's been pretty preoccupied with her new husband. She's also pregnant with twins."

"Twins? Wow. Do they run in your family?"

"My mother was Grant's twin." Grace, the evil twin.

Kerry ran her slender fingertips along the back of the sofa, causing Ford to have an immediate reaction down south. "I didn't have any brothers or sisters. I missed that growing up." Her wistful tone said she'd missed a lot of things and had faced more than her share of heartache.

"I have to admit, even though Abby's a pain in the butt sometimes, I wouldn't trade her."

She slid off her shoes and curled her legs beneath her. "What kind of parent was Grant?"

"He was tough but fair. He kept us in line. He also gave up a lot to raise us. Marriage and kids of his own."

"He was never seriously involved with a woman?"

"Not that we were aware of, although I'm sure he wasn't celibate all those years. Not many women to choose from in Crawley, but he did go out of town every now and then, leaving Buck in charge."

Kerry frowned. "Who's Buck?"

"He's our ranch foreman. Been there as long as I can remember. He started working for my great-grandparents as a teenager. He's as good as gold. Not exactly a pushover, but he let me and Abby get away with more than Grant ever did. Especially Abby. God, he loves her." Ford smiled with remembrance of Abby climbing into Buck's lap for a tall tale, and eventually teaching him to read. "In Buck's eyes, she can do no wrong. In fact, he's the reason she became a veterinarian. He basically taught her everything she knows about treating cattle and horses."

"Is he married?"

"Nope."

"You were brought up by a couple of confirmed bachelors who had to go out of town to find their women."

"That about sums it up."

"Does all of that apply to you? I mean, did you go out of town to find women?"

He wasn't sure he wanted to get into that at the moment. "I'm not celibate, either, if that's what you're asking. But I haven't had many long-term relationships. Most women don't consider living on a farm in the middle of nowhere a great lifestyle."

"I think it sounds intriguing," she said. "What's it like?"

Ford told Kerry about the hard work, hard living but most important, the rewards of owning and cultivating the land. She listened with sincere interest when he revealed he'd developed his own special feed and leased the patents globally, laughed when he told her about his and Abby's antics, and remained silent as he talked about his uncle's commitment to them.

"I'm glad you had Grant," she said after a long bout of silence. "It's hard having to deal with a mother's death."

Ford braced for the last of the revelations. "My mother isn't dead. She left me and Abby when we were in grade school. We haven't heard from her since. All I know is that she ran off with some kind of salesman."

"Is your father dead?"

He tipped his head back against the sofa and studied the ceiling. "I have no idea who he is. As far as I'm concerned, Grant is my dad."

When he felt the gentle touch on his shoulder, Ford turned his head to see compassion reflecting in her eyes. "I'm really sorry, Ford. Sounds like you've had it about as tough as I have."

"Not really," he said, resisting the urge to pull her into his arms. "I've always had a place to come home to."

Taking him by surprise, she scooted closer and took his hand. "That doesn't discount what your mother did to you. It hurts like hell, knowing a parent has such little regard for their child. In your case, children."

He laced his fingers with hers and gave her hand a squeeze. "Yeah, well I guess some people just aren't meant to be parents."

Their eyes met and held for a long moment, suspending Ford between a strong yearning to kiss her and blaring caution buzzing around in his head. Yearning was beginning to win out until another knock sounded at the door, sending Ford off the sofa to answer the summons.

A lanky waiter rolled in a cart containing their limited dinner, and Ford instructed him to put the food on the coffee table. The guy looked at Ford like he was some hayseed, which in many ways he was. But when he tipped him well, the man's attitude changed immediately. He couldn't be more accommodating, groveling all the way out of the room.

After he returned to Kerry, Ford ate his sandwich in record time, realizing he was hungrier than he'd thought. Obviously, she had restored his appetite, in more ways than one. He pushed aside the plate and leaned back, hands laced behind his neck, to watch Kerry nibble at her cheesecake.

"Is your feed business lucrative?" she asked, following another small bite.

He was more interested in watching her mouth than talking, engaging it in something other than everyday conversation. "I do fairly well. It enabled me to build my own house, complete with all the modern conveniences."

She sent him a teasing look. "No water wells and outdoor plumbing?"

"Water well, yes. Outhouse, no. But I do have a pool."

"Wow. That's great, and so is this cheesecake. Want to try it?"

"Sure."

As soon as she had the fork poised at his mouth, the cheese-cake took a dive, rolled down his bare chest and ended up in his lap. "I'm sorry," Kerry said, followed by an uncomfortable laugh.

"No problem." For Ford, it was somewhat of a problem, especially when he fantasized about her licking her way down his torso to clean up the sticky path.

Instead, Kerry grabbed a napkin, dipped it in a glass of water then worked over the spot. When she reached his groin, he caught her wrist. "I wouldn't do that if I were you."

She looked down, then back up at him, awareness as well as a faint shade of pink on her pretty face. "Oh. Sorry again."

Ford took the napkin from her, picked up the bite of dessert, rolled it up into the cloth and tossed it onto the table. "No harm done." Not much, although even the ice water hadn't helped his predicament. He was hard as a harrow and couldn't do a damn thing about it.

"Want to try it again?" she asked.

Oh, yeah, he did. He wanted to take up where they'd left off the night before. "If you mean the cheesecake, no."

In spite of the absence of wisdom, he took her hand, laid the fork on the tray, then pulled her against his side.

"Friendship, Ford," she said, but didn't try to move, even when he rubbed his hands down her bare arms.

"I'm just trying to warm you up. You're covered in goose bumps."

"I know, but I'm not cold."

"What are you, Kerry?"

A breathy sigh drifted from her lips. "Crazy for being here. Crazy for wanting you to kiss me again. For wanting you, period."

She didn't have to tell him twice before Ford took full advantage of her sweet lips. He tried to be gentle, keep it light, but the rush went straight to his head, causing him to conduct a very thorough, very deep investigation of her mouth.

Without thought, he lifted her up to straddle his lap. Kerry didn't issue a complaint, didn't pull away from him at all. In fact, she responded to the kiss without hesitation, and he welcomed that. Welcomed her hands coming to rest on his chest. Even welcomed his erection as she moved her bottom against his lap even knowing he couldn't do a damn thing about it. Totally on edge, he kept his hands at her waist and fought the temptation to touch her everywhere. Yet temptation won out when she moaned against his mouth and the glide of her hips against his groin grew more insistent.

Keeping his mouth firmly mated with hers, Ford used both hands to push her skirt up her legs, knowing full well that she needed something from him, something he was more than glad to give her. What he'd almost given her last night.

He waited a few moments, allowing her the opportunity to stop him, which she didn't. Instead, she dug her nails into his shoulders, played her tongue against his in a suggestive rhythm, exploring his mouth without reservation, exactly what he planned to do with her body, if she let him.

He lifted her bottom from his lap with one hand and with the other tugged the skirt up around her waist then pushed her panties down to the tops of her knees. Only then did he break the kiss and waited for her permission before he continued. He stroked the back of his knuckles below her navel and slid his free hand beneath the back of her shirt. "I want to touch you, Kerry. I have to touch you."

She locked into his gaze and murmured, "Ford, I need—"

"I know what you need, and I want you to know how it can be with a man who only wants to make you feel good." He traced circles above the golden vee between her legs. "But you only have to tell me no, and I'll stop."

She released a shaky breath, her unfocused eyes locked on his eyes. "This is insane."

He slid his hand lower, but not exactly where he wanted to be. "If you say yes, I'll make you crazy in a damn good way."

She closed her eyes and sighed. "Yes. Make me crazy."

*Yes* was exactly what he'd wanted to hear. *Yes* was all it took to proceed. He turned his palm and cupped her between her thighs then gently slid one fingertip through the damp folds. She bucked when he hit home, but she didn't bolt from his lap. Instead, she tipped her forehead against his to watch him touch her. Ford did the same, totally caught up in the erotic scene—Kerry with a leg on each side of his thighs, completely open to him, his hand in motion between her legs. He made methodical passes over her swollen flesh, intent on giving her a mind-blowing climax like she'd never known. His erection strained painfully against his jeans, and he considered opening his own fly to provide much-needed comfort. But he didn't want to stop until he'd given her what she needed. He also didn't want her believing he had to have more. This was for her benefit. All for her.

When Kerry pushed against his hand, Ford increased the pressure of his strokes and slid one finger inside her. He felt the beginnings of her orgasm, slightly at first then stronger and stronger. A sound caught somewhere between a moan and a whimper slipped out of her mouth. He captured that sound with his mouth, gliding his tongue in sync with the movement of his fingertip while he experienced every wave of her climax. He fantasized about how she would feel when he was buried inside her, almost at his own peril.

Kerry collapsed against him, her cheek now resting against his chest while he rubbed her back as he considered whether he should ask her to come to his bed. That wouldn't be a good idea, he decided. He sure as hell didn't want to rush her and risk she would turn away from him again. He would have to be satisfied knowing that someday soon he might have the opportunity to show her how it could be between a man and a woman when no force was involved.

But he wasn't completely satisfied, his only excuse for holding her face in his palms and saying, "Stay with me tonight, Kerry."

Without responding, she pulled her panties and skirt back into place, scooted off his lap, then turned around on the sofa, her gaze fixed on some unknown point across the room. "I can't, Ford. I know that's selfish on my part, considering what you've done for me tonight, but I'm just not ready yet. In fact, I shouldn't have allowed any of this to happen."

He understood what she was saying, and he didn't blame her. Still, he had to tell her what was on his mind. "Kerry, I know you're still dealing with my deception, but whether or not I told the truth about my identity, I still want to be with you. And I know you want to be with me, too. You proved that just a minute ago."

She sighed. "That wasn't exactly me. I'm usually very cautious."

"You were very hot. And you make me that way." He had half a mind to take her hand and show her. He chose to tell her. "I'm so turned on right now I could make love with you all night. And I know it would be so damn good between us. But I also know that's probably too much to ask of you right now. I'm willing to be patient and let you decide if and when."

Clasping his hand, she pulled it up and held it above her breasts, against her pounding heart. "Ford, there's something you have to know."

His immediate thought was she'd been lying about her relationship with Spencer. "What is it?"

A flash of pain reflected from her eyes. "I've tried to be

intimate with other men, but it's been difficult. You're the first one I've allowed to be that close to me since…" Her voice faltered along with her gaze.

He tipped her chin toward him so she could see how badly he hurt for her. "You may not believe this, but I do understand what you went through. And I hate like hell you had to go through it."

Although Abby hadn't suffered Kerry's fate, Ford had witnessed firsthand what her personal experience had done to his sister in terms of her relationships with men, and that made Kerry's situation all the more troublesome. He wanted to be a man she could trust. He wanted to prove to her he wouldn't hurt her in any way.

Kerry laid her head against his shoulder, their joined hands resting on his thigh, no more words passing between them. Ford enjoyed having her so close, relaxed and seemingly content, even if his own body still burned for her. But he had to take it easy, not be too persistent. And maybe, just maybe, he would have his opportunity to make love with her. Even if that didn't happen, he'd never regret knowing her. He *would* regret having to leave her.

"Did they ever catch the bastard who assaulted you?" he asked after a time.

She sighed. "No. It was dark in the alley, and I couldn't see his face. I couldn't identify him."

He released her hand and wrapped an arm around her shoulder, all he could think to do. He said, "I'm sorry, Kerry," all he could think to say.

"It was a long time ago," she said before raising her head to look at him again, an all-too-apparent ache in her eyes. "I'd be lying if I said I didn't carry a few internal scars from the experience along with the external ones. But when I met you, I decided it was time to take a few risks because I trusted you."

"And then I blew it when I lied to you."

She shrugged. "That's all behind us now. Maybe we should just start over."

Ford could accept that, as long as she was willing to be with him for however many days he had left in this city. "I agree."

"And that means I have to have time to decide how far I want this thing between us to go."

She had to learn to trust him all over again, he realized. "I'll give you all the time you need."

"Speaking of time." She checked her watch. "I really do have to go, otherwise I'll have a hard time getting up in the morning."

"I'm going to have a hard time all night." Ford wanted to take back the comment the minute it jumped out of his mouth. Old habits were damn difficult to break.

Thankfully, Kerry smiled. "I'm sure you'll handle things just fine."

He wanted her to handle "things," but from this point forward, she would have to take the initiative. "I'll manage."

When Kerry left the sofa, Ford came to his feet, hating that she was leaving. He followed her to the door, and once there she turned to face him with a smile. "What do you have planned for tomorrow?"

"I have an appointment with Grant's attorney to see where we stand."

Her smile faded as if she suddenly remembered he was still fighting for his uncle's very survival. Ford had to admit, at times he'd forgotten, too, especially when she'd been in his arms. That served to play up his guilt even more. "I'll stop by after work tomorrow, if that's okay," she said.

That was more than okay with him. "I look forward to it. Maybe we can go someplace to eat that doesn't serve hotel food."

"I'll keep that in mind, and I'll see you then." She walked out the door before he had a chance to kiss her again. Walked out before he could issue another lame apology. Before he tried to invite her once more into his lonely bed.

Ford would keep her in mind all night long, all day tomorrow until she came back to him, and probably long after he left godforsaken California.

# Six

**E**ventually Ford would be leaving California, a thought that kept playing over and over in Kerry's mind as she tried to work. Adding to her lack of concentration was the remembrance of her lack of inhibition last night, Ford's gentle skill, the absolute pleasure of his touch. Even now she shivered, twitched in the rigid office chair, feeling the effects as if it had happened only a few moments ago, not hours before.

Right now she had to think about her less-than-exciting job, filling in for a vacationing accounting clerk, and on a Monday, no less. Being stuck at a cluttered desk, inputting financial figures, wasn't nearly as exciting as the thought of escaping the doldrums to be with Ford. And that meant to be with him in every way.

Of course, she'd had the prime opportunity the evening before, but she'd squandered that because of a mix of mistrust and fear. At least she was beginning to understand him more,

and that included why he'd lied to her. Granted, she didn't care
for his dishonesty, but she did comprehend it. His obvious love
for his uncle had been more than apparent. He would do anything to protect his family. As Millie had said, there was a lot
of honor in that.

She also recognized that after she'd bared her soul, he had-
n't pressured her for more intimacy. But that intimacy issue
was first and foremost on her mind. She was just beginning
to recognize her own needs, a positive step in the right direction. Most men she'd dated in the past had walked away thinking her aloof, unattainable, which she had been. Until now.
Until Ford Ashton had come into her life with the promise of
showing her the power of her own sexuality, and she couldn't
ignore her desire to let him take her wherever he would.

She deserved to be whole again, and she inherently knew
Ford could help her on her way. She wasn't looking for him
to save her because that would be unrealistic. But she'd arrived at the point where if she didn't have all of him, and soon,
she was in danger of going up in a carnal blaze of glory. Some
might consider her a fool for even considering such a thing,
but Kerry liked to think of it as being a fair exchange. She
could offer him her friendship, and he could offer her an experience the likes of which she'd never known. For once, a
good experience. No. A *great* experience.

Kerry glanced at the clock on the wall, noting it was only
9 a.m., still three hours away from lunch and eight hours
away from Ford. Tonight she planned to take it to the limit by
taking Ford up on his offer to stay with him. First she had to
get busy, even though she'd rather eat pure horseradish than
to return to the dull data entry.

"Would you please take care of this, Kerry?"

Glancing up from the computer, Kerry forced a smile at the

oh-so-cocky Mona Gilbert—or Hormona, as the office girls like to call her—the newly appointed admin to the interim CEO. "Take care of what?"

"This." Mona tossed a pink message note in front of Kerry. "The post office keeps calling. They need you to pick up some mail that I presume didn't get routed to the office after Mr. Ashton's death. I don't have time to deal with it."

Like Kerry had the time. "Fine. I'll get it at lunch."

"See that you do." Mona swayed away, taking with her the stifling scent of overpowering fruity perfume as well as her arrogance. Too bad she hadn't worked for Spencer. They would have gotten along just great. Two peas in the proverbial pod. Bed buddies. Yuck.

Kerry tossed the note aside and sighed, cheek resting on her palm. So much for a relaxing lunch hour. She would grab a sandwich, pick up the mail and then return to her riveting work. Or she could pick up the mail, forget the sandwich and grab Ford.

Kerry suddenly decided that was a great option. In fact, she made another decision, as well. She had two weeks' worth of vacation coming. The company could do without her for a few days. She would finish out the morning, then present the excuse that something dire had come up at home, and spend the time getting to know Ford better. Getting to know all of him, before he was permanently out of her life. And try to help him with his goal to clear Grant. Of course, that meant leaving Millie alone, but Kerry could remedy that with one phone call to Millie's niece. It could also mean getting in too deep, heart first. Worth the risk, as far as Kerry was concerned.

Pumped up on anticipation, she began keying data at a record pace, mentally chanting, "Three more hours until lunch." Three more hours until Ford.

* * *

Ford spent the best part of Monday morning sitting in an upscale office waiting for Grant's attorney. Shortly before noon, Edgar Kent finally rushed into the room.

"Sorry I'm late, Mr. Ashton," he said as he extended his hand to Ford for a quick shake. "Busy morning."

Ford sat back down at the chair across from Kent's desk, tempted to tell him apology not accepted. Instead he asked, "What's going on with my uncle's case?"

Kent scooted his rolling chair beneath the desk and forked a hand though his silver hair. "Right now we're waiting for the grand jury to convene to hear his case."

"When will that be?"

He moved aside some documents to uncover a file and flipped it open. "Probably not until next week, maybe later."

That sure as hell wouldn't do. "And Grant has to waste away in jail until then?"

Kent closed the file and folded his hands on top of it. "If the grand jury finds that the evidence supports holding him over until trial, then he could be in for a long stay in jail. He'll be arraigned again if that happens, and I'll request bail again, but I'm not counting on having that granted."

Ford leaned back and released a rough sigh. "Do you think the evidence will hold out?"

"The witness who says he saw your uncle entering the building the night of Spencer Ashton's death is fairly compelling, especially since he picked him out of a lineup."

"Who is this witness?"

"I only have a name right now, but I'll be interviewing him when the time comes."

Ford leaned forward, his hands gripped tightly on the chair's arms. "Why don't you let me interview him? Because he's damn sure wrong about Grant."

Kent scowled. "The last thing we need is to have you harassing a witness. You need to allow the justice system to work."

Ford let go a cynical laugh. "Justice? What justice? An innocent man's sitting behind bars right now. That's not justice. That's immoral as hell."

Kent tented his fingers beneath his chin. "Mr. Ashton, you have to understand that your uncle doesn't have a good alibi other than he supposedly returned to Napa. No one saw him return. Spencer's assistant heard him threaten Spencer earlier that day. So he had motive, as well. The police know that he leaked the information of your grandfather's bigamy to the press. They also know he attempted to see him several times before they finally did meet."

"They don't know him at all. My uncle wouldn't kill anyone, even if the bastard did deserve to die. If Grant said he went back to Napa, then he did."

"Yet he has no proof he did return."

Ford leveled a hard stare on the man. "Are you saying even you don't believe him?"

Kent shifted under Ford's continued scrutiny. "It's not my job to believe him. It's my job to represent him to the best of my ability."

"And I just put down one helluva retainer for you to do just that." He came to his feet, no longer trusting he could keep his anger in check. "In the meantime, I'm going to keep digging until I find out who did this. And you're going to do whatever it takes to get him out of that hell hole."

With that, Ford turned away but before he could leave, Kent called him back. He turned around to find the attorney holding out a folded piece of yellow legal paper. "This is from your uncle. He asked me to give this to you."

Ford crossed the room, took the paper and slipped it

into the jacket's inside pocket. "Thank you. I'll be in touch."

On the way out, Ford was tempted to read the letter in the elevator but decided to wait. He considered reading it in the cab but the trip to the hotel was practically over before it had begun. But when he entered the hotel room, alone with his anger and frustration, he shucked off his jacket, sat on the sofa and finally unfolded the page. And soon his fury was replaced by a sadness the likes of which Ford had never known.

Ford,

I don't know what's going to happen to me, so I need to tell you a few things. First, keep your nose clean. Don't do anything that's going to get you into trouble, although I know you're probably bent on getting me out of here. Second, take good care of Abby in my absence, like you've always done. I know she has Russ now, but she still needs you, too. I'd hate to think I wouldn't be around to see the babies, but that's a possibility.

And in case you're wondering if I regret having to raise you and your sister, I wouldn't trade that time for anything in the world. Not even for my freedom right now. You two are the best things that ever happened to me, and although I hate like hell what Grace did to you, in a way she did me a favor. And now I'm going to ask a couple of favors from you.

First, don't let what your mother did to you keep you from trying to find the right woman. Second, when you have the time, check on Anna Sheridan. She became a good friend while I was at The Vines. Just tell her I'm going to be okay and she will be, too.

Last, I probably didn't tell you enough while you were growing up, bud, but I'm telling you now. I love you and Abby, more than I love my own life. Just keep remembering that, no matter what happens.

Grant.

Ford tossed the letter aside, laid his head back and closed his eyes. The last time he'd cried, he'd been eight years old and Grant had told him his mother had left. He never let anyone see those tears because he'd cried them at night in his bed. Since that time, he'd been determined to be the consummate tough guy, the one who had no use for emotions. Had no use for feelings in general because it was just much easier to feel numb.

Right then he came as close to crying as he had since that day. Tightening his jaw, he fought the emotions as fervently as he fought to save his uncle. Fought not to feel at all. Regardless, he experienced the keen bite of sorrow mixed with the fury over the unfairness of Grant's situation.

He needed a strong drink, but alcohol would only cloud his head. He needed to think about what to do next. Most of all, he needed someone to talk to. And that someone was Kerry Roarke.

Kerry stood at Ford's hotel door, barely able to contain her excitement. She'd cut out of the office at 11:00 a.m., gone by the house and packed a bag while Millie was out for her Monday bridge game, and then she dropped by the post office. The final stopover had led to the discovery of something she hadn't expected. Something very encouraging. It might not mean anything in the grand scheme of things, but it could very well be the key to clearing Grant Ashton. And she couldn't wait to tell Ford the news.

Yet when Ford answered her summons after two knocks, Kerry's excitement faded into deep concern. He looked totally weary and wasted. His hair was ruffled, as if he'd run his hands through it several times, his eyes reddened, turning them an even brighter shade of blue. He simply stared at her for a moment, and without speaking, Kerry dropped the nylon tote and her purse at her feet and walked into his arms. He held on to her tightly, as if she had become his lifeline. She welcomed that he needed her right then, even if she didn't welcome his obvious despair.

After a time he dropped his arms from around her and stepped back, looking somewhat self-conscious. "You're early."

"I hope that's not a problem."

"Not at all. I've never been so glad to see anyone in my life."

Kerry could say the same for herself. She'd imagined this moment all morning, although she hadn't imagined how great he would look in a white tailored shirt, pushed up at the sleeves, and a pair of form-fitting navy slacks. Nor had she imagined he would look so discouraged. Hopefully she could help ease that with her news.

He pointed to the bag at her feet. "What's in there?"

"A change of clothes in case I need them later." Several changes of clothes, but she decided to save that information until later.

He gestured toward the living area. "Come in and I'll tell you how my sorry morning went."

Kerry picked up her belongings and moved into the room, allowing Ford to close the door. She headed to the sofa while Ford walked to the wet bar in the corner and poured a cup of coffee. Without looking at her, he said, "Do you want a cup?"

"No, thanks. I've had more than my share today." Kerry set her things on the coffee table, dropped onto the sofa and waited until Ford settled beside her before saying, "I take it things didn't go well with the attorney."

He took a drink of coffee, then let go a rough sigh. "You

could say that. He pretty much told me there's not a lot that can be done. The evidence against Grant is strong. He's been identified in a lineup and he had motive. All I can do is wait and hope something breaks in the case, although I don't know what that something could be."

"Maybe I do." Kerry rummaged through her purse and withdrew two pieces of mail and held them up for Ford's inspection.

He set his coffee cup down on the end table. "What is that?"

"Mail for Spencer from his private P.O. box. I'd forgotten all about it until I got the message this morning these needed to be picked up."

"Do the police know about this P.O. box?"

"I'm not sure. As far as I know, Spencer had the only key. I only went there one time because he was too busy. I received strict instructions not to open anything. That's why I've always assumed he rented it so he could receive love letters from his latest girl-of-the-month."

"So are they love letters?"

"Not exactly." She slipped the paper from the longest envelope, unfolded it and handed it to him. "That's a bank statement. Best I can tell, it's a biannual recap of transactions, beginning last January. You'll notice that every month this year until May, he deposited ten thousand dollars, and the funds were withdrawn in the same month."

Ford studied the statement for a moment. "I'm not sure what this proves."

"Maybe nothing without this."

She handed him the letter from the second envelope and allowed him time to read it, which he did out loud. "'If you stop paying me, you will pay one way or another.'" His gaze zipped to hers. "Someone was blackmailing him."

"That's my guess. Question is, who is that someone? And did they murder him?" Kerry showed him the empty envelope. "It has an Oakland postmark dated in May, but no return address. Whoever sent this was in the vicinity at the time of Spencer's death."

Ford slid his hands through his hair. "Yeah, and that means Grant, too. This could implicate him if they believe he was doing the blackmailing."

"Regardless, we have to turn it over to the police."

"I know that, but I want to wait a day or two."

"Why?"

"Because I have something else I need to check out." Ford leaned over and picked up a piece of legal pad paper from the coffee table. "This is a letter from Grant. Read it."

Kerry took the page and read it silently, her eyes soon clouding with a mist of tears that threatened to fall when she comprehended the depth of Grant Ashton's commitment to his nephew. No wonder Ford was so distraught. No wonder he was fiercely determined to clear his uncle. "Do you think he's giving up?"

"Grant's a strong man, physically and mentally. I wouldn't believe he would ever give up. But then, I have no idea what he's going through right now. I'm not sure I want to know, because it would probably kill me."

Kerry laid a comforting hand on his arm. "You can't give up, either, Ford. We'll keep trying as long as it takes to see him out of jail."

"I plan to, and I've been wondering about something else." He pointed to a passage near the end. "I know this is probably a long shot, but do you know anything about this Anna Sheridan?"

More than she'd wanted to know. "As a matter of fact, I do. Her sister, Alyssa, used to be Spencer's assistant." And mistress. "I replaced her because she was pregnant. She died not long after the baby was born and now Anna is raising him. That baby is Spencer's son."

Ford tossed the mail onto the table and leaned forward. "Damn. The man knew no shame when it came to screwing up people's lives. First he leaves my grandmother high and dry to raise his kids alone. Then he jilts Caroline out of the family company and fathers four more kids he practically abandoned. Then he moves on to another woman and fathers three more. God only knows what he's done to them and his current wife, although I don't know anything about her or that branch of the Ashtons."

"Believe me, Ford, you don't want to know Lilah Ashton. I had to deal with her when she visited Spencer at Ashton-Lattimer. She's a shark."

Ford sent her a cynical smile. "Good. I hope she made his final years pure hell." He collapsed back against the couch. "I'm still wondering about Grant's connection to Anna. He says he met her at The Vines, but from the looks of the letter, I suspect they were closer that he's letting on. I'm kind of surprised he never mentioned her, but Grant can be fairly secretive about that sort of thing."

The cogs in Kerry's brain started turning. "I met Anna once when she brought the baby into the office and demanded to see Spencer. Spencer was in a meeting at the time, so she left, but she wasn't very happy about it. I'm sure she wasn't too thrilled when the press got wind that the little boy was Spencer's. More than likely they've made her life chaotic. I certainly know how that feels."

Ford's expression told her he truly sympathized. "I'm sure you do, and I'm also sorry you got caught up in all this mess."

Kerry put the letter next to the other mail and curled one leg beneath her. "Honestly, I feel guilty for telling the police about the argument I overheard between Spencer and your uncle. For months I had to turn him away, and he was always so nice to me, even though he was furious with Spencer. But that afternoon..." Her gaze drifted away along with her words. Confession might be good for the soul, but her soul was being ripped to shreds.

"What about that afternoon?"

Kerry looked up and met his gaze. "I felt sorry for Grant so I let him back without telling Spencer. If I hadn't done that, maybe none of this would have happened."

He touched her face and rubbed his thumb over her cheek. "Hey, it's not your fault. You were just trying to help Grant. And you had to tell the truth about the argument. You didn't have a choice."

Kerry appreciated his understanding more than she could express. "Any ideas on what to do next?" She had one in particular but felt it wouldn't be appropriate to present it. Not yet.

"I called Caroline earlier and told her I'd be driving to Napa this evening to see her. I want to find out what she knows about Anna and Grant's relationship."

So much for dinner plans. So much for all her lovemaking plans, at least for the time being. "That sounds like a good idea."

"Even more so now. From what you say, I can't help but wonder if maybe Grant's protecting Anna in some way. Maybe she was involved and he went back to the building to stop her."

"That could be. What time do you have to leave?"

"Caroline told me to be there around 6:30 for drinks and invited me to stay on for dinner. I've already rented a car."

Kerry smiled around her disappointment. "Another Mustang?"

"Actually, an SUV, and I'd like you to come with me, if you're game."

Oh, she was game, for that and much, much more. "Sure." She checked her watch. "It's twelve-thirty now, it takes about an hour and a half to get to Napa, so that leaves four and a half hours before we need to leave."

"Do you have to go back to work?"

Time to unveil the plan, and prepare for possible rejection. "Actually, I don't have to go back today. I don't have to go back until next Monday. I took the time off to spend it with you. As long as you don't object to having a roommate for the remainder of the week."

He looked positively shocked. "You want to stay here?"

"If you have room for me."

"I only have one bedroom, Kerry."

"I realize that."

"Do you want me to sleep on the couch?"

She released a ragged breath. "No, I want you to sleep with me. And not only to sleep."

Ford shifted on the cushions. "Are you sure?"

"Positive."

His expression went suddenly serious. "I'll be leaving eventually."

"I know, and I want to make the most of our time together. We've both been through a lot, past and present, and I don't think there's anything wrong with escaping together, even if only temporarily."

Ford stood and paced the room for a few moments. He seemed to be mulling over her words while Kerry seemed to stop breathing. If he refused, she would handle it. She wouldn't like it, but she'd deal with it.

Finally he stopped and stood before her, his expression no less somber. "One question."

"Okay."

"Do you still have that condom?"

Kerry smiled from relief and anticipation and just plain giddiness. "I can go one better than that." Leaning down, she rifled through the bag, pulled out the box and tossed it into his hands. "I believe in being prepared."

He turned the condom box over then nailed her with a devastating grin, emphasizing his gorgeous dimples. "This should be enough to last us tonight."

Kerry kicked off her shoes and shed her tailored black blazer. The rest she would leave for him to remove. After coming to her bare feet, she circled her arms around him.

"I don't want to wait until tonight."

"You want to make love now?" His voice was hoarse and incredibly deep.

"Yes. I need to see your face in the daylight."

Comprehension showed in his expression. "Anything you want I'll do it. You only have to ask me."

"I can tell you one thing I don't want, Ford."

"What's that?"

"I don't want you to treat me like I'm fragile, because I'm not. As far as I'm concerned, this is the first time for me, and I don't want you to hold anything back, and neither will I." She brushed a kiss across his lips. "I want you to treat me like you would any other woman."

She wasn't like any other woman he'd ever known—Ford's first thought as they stood in the bedroom, tossing away clothes like dried leaves caught in a wind current. His second thought centered on slowing down, the reason why he left her panties and his briefs intact, for now.

Without bothering to turn down the spread, Ford took Kerry down on the bed. He held her face in his palms and kissed her, trying desperately to stay grounded. That seemed almost impossible when she stroked her tongue against his and moved her hips beneath him. After breaking the kiss, he rolled to his side and ran one fingertip along her throat then over the rise of her breast.

The light streaming in from the window allowed him to see all the details as he touched her, and that alone was almost more than he could take. Lowering his head, he flicked his tongue over one nipple, then the other. She slid her hands in his hair as if she might be anchoring herself, as well.

He raised his head to watch her, keeping his gaze centered on hers as he slid his finger slowly down her belly. She trembled and a slight gasp slipped out of her mouth. Ford was on the verge of some serious shaking, too. But he vowed to keep it together for a while longer. He also vowed to pull out all the stops, at her request. He planned to crush out all her bad memories, and replace them with good ones. Beginning now.

Coming to his knees, he told her, "Lift up," and when she complied, he slid her panties down her legs and tossed them away.

Ford didn't know what he'd done in his lifetime to deserve this, seeing Kerry lying there, looking so damn beautiful. He'd viewed his share of nude women, but he'd never been as moved by any of them. Her hair formed a golden halo on the pillow still covered by the burgundy spread. Her face was flushed a slight shade of pink that almost matched the color of her nipples. Her breasts were full, her curves generous, her legs long and made to wrap around his waist when he made love to her. She was a mix of saint and seductress, and he wanted her so badly he almost couldn't think.

His gaze wandered down to the light shading between her thighs and every muscle in his body clenched in an effort to maintain control. Overpowering need had him considering parting her legs and sinking inside her. Common sense took hold and told him to focus only on her. To make sure she was more than ready to take the next step.

Regardless that she'd told him not to hold back, he still felt the need to tell her what he intended to do. On that thought, he snaked out of his briefs, stretched out beside her again and pushed her hair back from her ear to whisper, "I want to kiss you. Everywhere."

She turned her face toward him. "I want you to do that, as long as you let me return the favor."

Since that request hadn't totally sent him over the edge, Ford realized he was a lot stronger than he'd believed. He touched his lips to hers and pulled back to study her face. "I want you to do that, but I'm barely hanging on here."

She gave him a shaky smile. "I understand. Later, then."

Later worked fine for Ford, and no way would she understand how he felt at that moment. He didn't understand it himself. But here and now held the most importance. He worked his lips down her body, placing a light kiss on each of her breasts, another above her navel, before he bent her knees and positioned himself between her legs. Sliding his hands beneath her bottom, he lifted her slightly to meet his mouth.

Kerry drew in a sharp breath when he reached his goal, much the same as she had last night. He kept the pull of his lips light, the stroke of his tongue steady until she moved her hips in a telling rhythm. Only then did he slide one finger inside her, determined to feel the surge of her climax. It hit her fast, hit her strong and in turn served to increase the heaviness and strength of Ford's erection. He couldn't remember when he'd needed someone so badly. Needed to be inside her. Needed to hold her close to his pounding heart.

In a matter of moments, he would be exactly where he wanted to be, as close to Kerry as he could possibly be. And he inherently knew that by doing so, he could be forever lost in her. To her.

# Seven

**T**rembling, Kerry kept her eyes closed as she tried to recover from the impact of the orgasm. Her mind fought the voyage back to earth, but her body told her she needed more. She was mildly aware of Ford leaving the bed and the sound of tearing paper. She was very aware when he skimmed his taut body up her body. She welcomed his weight. Welcomed his intense kiss. Welcome the feel of every ridge and muscle against her palms as she sent her hands on a journey over his back and bottom.

He slid one hand in her hair and slipped the other between them, nudging her legs apart with his thigh. "Look at me, sweetheart."

Sweetheart. At one time she might have found that archaic, but not with Ford. Such a simple endearment said with a world of emotion. She opened her eyes to his beautiful face illuminated by the light of day and the heat of desire. His eyes were bright and oh, so blue and he kept them fixed on her eyes as he pushed inside her. She felt no pain, no fear, only full-ness. Completeness, as well, both at the place where they were now joined and deep in her heart.

He tipped his head against her shoulder, and she felt a slight shudder running through him.

"Ford?" Her voice sounded unsure, exactly how she felt at the moment.

He raised his head and traced her lips with a fingertip. "You feel so incredible."

"So do you." And he did, so very, very good.

He looked concern, and she loved him for that. "Are you sure?"

"Positive."

"I don't want to hurt you."

She could tell by the hard set of his jaw that he was fight-ing his natural instinct. And Kerry would have none of that. "You won't hurt me." She ran her tongue along the seam of his lips. "So don't hold back."

Those simple words unleashed something inside of Ford that both thrilled and excited Kerry. He moved inside her slowly at first, then harder and wilder. Touched her every-where, including the place that his mouth had so tenderly ma-nipulated only moments before.

She relished every sensation—the power of his body in motion, the feel of his hair-roughened legs entwined with hers, the strength of his broad back beneath her palms, his whispered words of praise so soft at her ear. The way it should be, she recognized, a mutual joining with a seductive and skillful man. A man who didn't know the meaning of brute force but instead knew how to treat a woman.

Then one sensation overtook all others, the onset of an-other release bearing down upon her. She lost track of place

and time until the steady pulse began to subside. Ford tensed
in her arms and muttered an oath that Kerry considered the
most sexy thing she'd ever heard leave a man's mouth. His
breath rode out on a long hiss, followed by a low groan. He
claimed her mouth with a drugging kiss, his hands still in
motion over her body, and hers roving over his. They remained that way for a long time, kissing and touching and
holding on to each other, as if they couldn't quite get enough
of the contact. Kerry wondered if she would ever get enough
of him.

Still joined to her body, Ford smiled, both his dimples and
eyes shining. "Damn, that was great," he muttered, bringing
about Kerry's laugh.

"I have to agree," she said.

"No regrets?"

She palmed his jaw. "None at all. Thank you."

"No. Thank you."

They kissed some more, touched some more until Ford finally rolled onto his side with Kerry still securely in his arms.
She kept her head nestled against his chest until she heard his
breathing grow steady and deep. That sound, along with the
solid beat of his heart, lulled her into sleep. She didn't know
how long she'd been out when she awoke to find Ford had
flipped onto his belly, his face turned toward her.

Kerry grabbed the opportunity to take in all the little details, beginning with his features now slack in sleep, his brown
lashes fanning below his closed lids, the deep bow of his lips
and the tiny cleft in his chin. She studied his arm covered in
golden hair contrasting with his tanned skin, his large hand
spanning the pillow next to his face. She visually scanned his
back, broad and bronzed, and kept going right down his spine
to his incredible butt. Incredible bronzed butt. He had absolutely no tan line at all. Anywhere.

Somehow, someway, the man maintained an allover tan. Kerry seriously doubted it was product-enhanced, because it looked too natural. She supposed he might drive a tractor in the nude, but that seemed highly unlikely. Yet the vision caused a giggle to bubble up in her throat and threaten to explode into a laugh. Before that occurred, she decided to take a shower and let him sleep a while longer.

Kerry made quick work in the bath, hoping the hotel hair dryer didn't wake Ford. But when she left the room, she discovered he hadn't moved an inch. After checking the clock, she realized she probably should wake him. Otherwise they would be late for their dinner in Napa.

Perched on the edge of the bed in a lush terry robe provided by the hotel, Kerry watched Ford again while she ran a brush through her hair. When she cleared her throat and he still didn't rouse, she patted his bare bottom and said, "Time to get up, Farmer Ford."

His eyes drifted open and he came fully awake with a grin. "You smell good." His voice was grainy and gruff and so patently sexy that Kerry considered shedding the robe and forgetting about everything but him.

"And you sleep very soundly," she said.

He rolled onto his back, totally secure in his nudity, and ran a palm down his torso, from chest to belly. Even though Kerry should be totally satisfied and sexually sated, she felt the familiar stirrings of wet heat between her thighs, sensations she had denied for too long. She certainly couldn't deny them now. If they had more time, she just might suggest they do something about her need, and Ford's, which had grown very obvious right before her eyes.

His grin deepened as he slid his hand lower as if to taunt her. "Something else is coming awake."

Kerry pushed off the bed and stood. "I see that." Boy, did she.

Crooking his finger at her, he said, "Why don't you come over here and give me a good-afternoon kiss."

As tempting as that sounded, she didn't dare. Not if they intended to get on the road soon. "I'm thinking you should probably go shower before we keep Caroline waiting."

He laced his hands behind his neck and bent one leg at the knee. "I'm thinking we should be fashionably late."

She waved the brush at him as her heart rate did double time. "Now, now. That would be rude."

He glanced down and so did Kerry. "Considering my current state, I'm liable to embarrass both of us, unless we do something about it pretty soon."

Kerry considered his words, and although she was sorely tempted, she decided she would find the time to help him out when they had more time. "The quicker we learn about Anna Sheridan, the quicker we can plan what to do next. And the quicker we can get back here and settled in for the night."

Ford stared at the ceiling. "You're right. I can't forget about Grant or why I'm in San Francisco."

Kerry hated that she'd reminded him of that. Hated that his uncle's arrest was the only reason he was there and that after it was resolved he'd be gone again. "I left you a towel, so have fun with your shower."

He turned his blue eyes on her again. "I'd have more fun if you'd join me."

Again, temptation came calling, but logic won out. "We can do that later. Otherwise we will be late."

Following a sigh, Ford climbed out of the bed and thankfully headed to the bath. If he'd taken one step toward her, Kerry's resolve would have weakened and they might never leave the hotel room.

She watched him walk away, all the while admiring his muscled bottom flexing with each step, still intrigued by his allover tan. Before he closed the bathroom door, she said, "Ford, you don't have any tan lines."

He turned, one large hand braced on the jamb. "No, ma'am, I don't."

She crossed her legs against another rush of heat when her gaze drifted down the stream of hair below his navel and didn't stop there. After forcing her gaze back to his face, she asked, "Care to explain?"

He smiled again. "There's something to be said for a pool and a privacy fence after coming in from the field at lunchtime. You just strip down, dive in, then lie around for an hour or so and daydream."

"What do you daydream about?"

"Nothing much, but I guarantee when I go back I'll be having some really nice ones about you."

With that he closed the door and left Kerry alone with another reminder of his imminent departure. She allowed herself a private daydream, one that involved living a simple life surrounded by simple people. Spending lazy days and endless nights with a gorgeous guy who was anything but simple. Never again having to worry about locking doors or dealing with big-city hassles.

And that seemed about as probable to Kerry Roarke as having a future with Ford Ashton.


When they arrived at The Vines, a housekeeper showed Ford and Kerry to the living room where they found Caroline waiting. She rose from a black chair and gave him a brief hug. "I'm glad you're here."

"Caroline, this is Kerry Roarke," he said. "She's been helping me out with details about the murder." Helping him out with a lot more.

If Caroline was at all surprised by Kerry's presence, Ford

couldn't tell from her relaxed smile. "Welcome to The Vines, Kerry."

Kerry took the hand Caroline offered for a polite shake. "Thank you for having me here." She looked around the room with an awed expression. "This is a beautiful place. Millie would love all the antiques."

"Millie is Kerry's landlady," Ford offered.

"Well, let's make ourselves comfortable," Caroline said, indicating a striped couch while she took a nearby chair.

Ford and Kerry sat on the sofa, keeping a decent berth between them. When he noticed Kerry wringing her hands, he fought the urge to take them into his hands to calm her nerves. Not a good idea. The less Caroline knew about their relationship, the better.

Caroline picked up a bottle of white wine from an ice bucket set out on the coffee table separating them and held it up. "Would either of you like a glass? It's one of our best Chardonnays."

Ford waved off the offer. "None for me. No offense, but I'm not much of a wine drinker."

"Would you prefer something else, Ford?" she asked.

Yeah, whiskey straight up from the bottle. "No, thanks. I'm driving."

"I'd love some wine," Kerry said.

She looked like she could use a drink, Ford decided. Or two or three. Maybe he shouldn't have brought her here, and he wasn't really sure why he'd thought that necessary. Easy. He didn't want to be away from her for any length of time.

Caroline poured a glass for Kerry, handed it to her and then took one for herself. She leaned back in the chair, looking every bit the refined lady, not a blond hair out of place or a single wrinkle in her pink suit. Kerry wore the clothes she had on from work, the skirt and blouse he'd gladly removed and would be glad to remove again later. With his jeans, boots and polo, he was definitely underdressed.

Caroline took a sip of her wine, then rested her hand on the arm of the chair. "You mentioned on the phone you had something you needed to ask me, Ford?"

He crossed one leg over the other and tried to loosen up. "Yeah. It's about Anna Sheridan."

"What about her?"

"I need to know what you know about her relationship with Grant."

Caroline frowned. "Why?"

"Because Grant sent a letter to me through Edgar Kent this morning. He mentioned her. In fact, he asked me to come here and tell her he's going to be okay."

Caroline took a small sip of the wine, keeping a firm grip on the glass. "I suppose they're only friends."

Ford wouldn't bet on that, considering Caroline's lack of conviction. "You didn't notice anything other than friendship going on between them?"

She leaned forward and topped off her glass. "To be honest with you, I've been distracted lately. My daughter Mercedes is having a few problems."

"Anything serious?" Ford asked.

"Boyfriend problems. It seems hers has suddenly disappeared. But that's the least of your worries. Are you suggesting that perhaps Anna and Grant were having some sort of tryst?"

Ford ran a hand over his jaw. "I don't know about that, but I find it kind of strange he asked about her. He's usually pretty guarded about that sort of thing."

Caroline raised a finely arched eyebrow. "You mean women?"

"Yeah. And the tone of the letter makes me wonder if he's

protecting her in some way. Maybe she's got something to do with Spencer's murder."

Caroline toyed with the pearls at her throat. "I can't imagine Anna would be involved in anything like that. Granted, she did try to confront Spencer at the estate and encountered Lilah, poor girl, and never got in to see him. That's how she ended up here with little Jack. She had nowhere else to go and frankly, she was afraid someone would hurt the baby after she started getting some threats on his life."

"Threats?" Kerry asked, the first word she'd spoken since they'd gotten past the pleasantries.

"Yes, and that's never been solved, but they've ended now."

As far as Ford was concerned, everything about this situation was growing more bizarre by the minute. "I'm guessing Spencer never claimed Jack."

"Of course not. Why would he bother?"

No reason to bother at all, Ford thought. "I need to talk to Anna. I have to know if she's hiding something."

"She's here, as far as I know," Caroline said. "She's staying at the cottage by the lake."

Ford stood. "You two have a nice visit. Hopefully this won't take too long."

When he felt a hand on his shoulder, Ford turned to see Kerry standing beside him. "Why don't you let me handle this, Ford?"

"Why would you want to do that?"

"I did meet her the time she came into Ashton-Lattimer, so I'm not a total stranger. I'm also a woman. If you charge in there and toss out presumed allegations based on theory, she's not going to talk to you."

Although she didn't say it, Ford knew exactly what Kerry was thinking. He'd nearly screwed up their relationship because of his preconceived notions about her. "Okay. I'll go with you."

"That's not necessary. I can give you a full report later." She turned to Caroline. "Mrs. Sheppard, the wine is wonderful. I would love to have another glass on my return, if that's okay."

"Of course it is, dear." Caroline stood and gestured toward the opening of the room. "Just go left and after you exit the rear of the house, follow the path to the right that leads to the cottage. If you have trouble, I'll have my husband escort you. He should be coming in at any moment for dinner."

"I have a good sense of direction, so I'm sure I'll find it without any problem. And please don't wait dinner on me. This could take a while."

Ford watched Kerry walk out, feeling somewhat powerless even though he trusted her to do whatever she could to aid Grant's cause. He also felt somewhat guilty when he realized he'd been following the movement of her hips in that skirt. Clearing his throat, he sat back down and said, "I think I'll have that drink now. Do you have any bourbon?"

"I certainly do." Caroline rose gracefully and walked to a decanter set atop some kind of a bureau across the room. "Ice?" she asked after she poured a highball glass full of the amber liquid.

"Nope. Straight up."

Caroline crossed the room, handed him the tumbler and this time sat beside him. "Kerry seems like a lovely girl. I'm not surprised Spencer hired her."

Ford took a long draw off the drink and welcomed the liquor burning down his throat. "He hired her, but he didn't have an affair with her."

Caroline looked at him curiously. "Are you absolutely sure?"

"Yeah. She hated him. And I believe her."

"Is that your head talking or your heart?"

"I don't know what you mean." He knew exactly what she'd meant, and he hated being that obvious in his admiration.

She gave him a knowing smile. "I've seen the way you look at her, and the way she looks at you. I sense quite a bit of mutual admiration between the two of you."

Ford stared at what was left of the booze in his glass. "Once I found out she had nothing to do with Spencer's murder, I realized I liked her a lot. Actually, I liked her before I found out. Crazy, huh?"

"No, not crazy at all. I understand completely. I knew I was in love with Lucas not long after we met."

In love? Ford sat back and drained the glass dry. "I didn't say that, Caroline."

"Love truly isn't so horrible, Ford. And you know, California isn't, either. It's really a rather nice place to live. Especially in the Napa area."

He knew where this was leading. Time to rein her in. "I have a farm. And a business. Abby's there. My life is there. In Nebraska, not California." Funny how he'd sounded like he was trying to convince himself as well as Caroline.

She didn't look the least bit ruffled. "Then perhaps you might consider taking a souvenir back with you."

Normally Ford might be angry over the less-than-subtle hints, but he couldn't be mad at Caroline. Playing dumb was his best defense. "Well, I thought about picking up some of those weird spices from Chinatown for Abby."

Caroline stared at him like she could see right through him. Probably because she could. "Ford, I hope that you don't let what your mother did ruin your chances of finding someone special. Not every woman is like her. And I hope you forgive me for trying to sound like your mother."

If only she had been his mother, then maybe his history with successful relationships might not be nonexistent. "I hear what you're saying, Caroline. But I just met Kerry. I have no idea how long I'll be here, and it's probably best to keep things light between us."

After a pat on his arm, she took her hand away and laced it with the other in her lap. "Of course, dear. You know what's best for you. I trust you'll find that special someone some day. Maybe sooner than you think."

Ford already had a special lady. Kerry Roarke was special in many ways. And he hadn't realized until that moment how much she'd begun to affect him. But he didn't care to confess that to Caroline—or even to himself.

Kerry knocked twice and was almost ready to give up when the door swung open to Anna Sheridan. "May I help you?"

A polite enough greeting, but Kerry noted the wariness in her brown eyes. "You probably don't remember me, but we've met before. Kerry Roarke, Spencer Ashton's former assistant."

"I remember you. Why are you here?"

From her distrustful tone, no doubt Anna believed Kerry had replaced her sister in every way. "If I could come in for a minute, I'll explain. It's important."

Anna didn't budge. "Can you at least give me a hint?"

"I have a message to give you from Grant Ashton."

Kerry immediately noticed the change in Anna. Her stern expression brightened and her shoulders seemed to slump, as if hearing Grant's name made her boneless. "You've seen Grant?"

"No, but his nephew, Ford, received a letter from him. I'm here on his behalf. And I promise this won't take long."

Finally Anna moved aside and allowed Kerry to enter a small living area decorated with rough-hewn furnishings and a lot of quilts. "Have a seat and I'll be right back," Anna told her before disappearing down a hallway.

Kerry took a seat on the sofa and nervously thrummed her fingers on the cushions as she prepared a mental laundry list of questions to present to Anna. She had to be kind, considerate and above all, cautious. Otherwise, Anna could very well boot her out before she had answers.

Anna returned shortly thereafter and sat on a small chair catty-corner to the sofa. "I've put the baby to bed early because he didn't have his nap today. He could wake up a few times before he's down for the night."

In other words, make it quick, Kerry. "I understand. First of all, Grant wants you to know he's going to be okay."

She looked away. "But he's not okay. He's still in jail."

"True, he is. But Ford's trying very hard to get him cleared."

"Anyone who came in contact with Spencer Ashton suffered for it." Her acid tone indicated the extent of Anna's hatred.

Discretion was definitely in order, Kerry decided. Otherwise, Anna might stop talking altogether. "I know. I worked for Spencer Ashton. He could be very charming. It's understandable why a woman like your sister would have fallen victim to that charm and suffered for it."

Anna finally brought her attention to Kerry. "But you didn't?"

"No. I'd heard about him through the office grapevine, and I knew immediately he couldn't be trusted. He was a master manipulator."

"How well I know. He definitely manipulated Alyssa." She leaned forward, a world-weary look on her face. "And I hold him responsible for her death. He wanted her to get rid of the baby, and when she wouldn't, he wrote her off completely. He didn't even have the decency to check on her when she called and told him she was in labor. By the time she got to the hospital, she was hemorrhaging. It's a miracle they saved Jack. But they couldn't save her. In a way, I think she gave up."

Although it was bad form to think ill of the dead, Kerry despised Spencer Ashton more now than she ever had. "I'm sorry, Anna. At least Jack has you now."

"I'm all that he has."

Which would give Grant prime motivation to protect her if, in fact, she was somehow involved in the murder. "Anna, I hate to ask this, but I have to know. Do you have any knowledge about what happened the night Spencer was murdered?"

Her shoulders tensed, but she failed to look at Kerry. "I don't know what you mean."

Oh, but she did. Kerry had become well versed at reading people, although Ford had been the exception. But in a way, she'd probably known he was hiding something; she just hadn't wanted to see it. Anna Sheridan was definitely hiding something.

"Did you have anything to do with his murder?"

Surprisingly, Kerry saw no anger in Anna's expression. "I hated him, but I would never risk leaving Jack alone. So the answer to your question is no. I did not kill Spencer Ashton, even though I never shed a tear over his death. And I am positive Grant didn't kill him, either." ·

"How do you know that for sure?"

"Because he was with me that night, all night, right here."

That was not what Kerry had been expecting. She hesitated for a moment, trying to regroup from the shock. "If that's true, why haven't you come forward?"

Anna's eyes welled with tears. "Because he told me not to. He was afraid for me and for Jack. Afraid for Jack because of some threats we received on his life. And afraid for me because he thought the police might believe we were in on the murder together. I asked him to let me tell them, but he made me promise I wouldn't." A few tears drifted down her cheeks, and she swiped them away with the back of her hand. "But I can't do it anymore. I'll come forward. I'll take a lie detector test if I have to. Anything to get him out of that horrible place."

Kerry considered going to her and giving her a hug, but Anna stiffened her frame and resumed her calm in short order. "So now you know the truth. If you'd like, I'll ask Caroline to stay with Jack and I'll go with you back into San Francisco to talk to the police tonight."

At the moment Kerry wished Ford were there to hear the truth and to advise her on what to do next. All she knew right then was Anna looked as if she might crumble in a mild wind. "One night isn't going to matter, Anna. I'll have Ford call you in the morning and arrange a time for you to come in to the police station. I'm sure he'll want to accompany you."

She pressed the heels of her palms against her eyes. "I can't stand the thought of Grant being in that place even one more hour, much less another night."

Unfortunately, Kerry was in the position to see the reality of the situation where Anna was not. "I seriously doubt they'll release him immediately."

"Why?"

"Because it's going to take time. I suspect they'll want to know why you waited to come forward, and they'll have quite a few questions." They really might believe she was in cahoots with Grant, a fact Kerry didn't feel Anna could handle at the moment.

Leaning over, Kerry pulled a tissue from the holder set out on the end table, stood and handed it to Anna. "Are you going to be okay in the meantime?"

Anna dabbed at her eyes, sniffed, then tucked her auburn hair behind her ears with one shaky hand. "Sure. I'll be fine. As long as I know Grant will finally get out, I'll take whatever might come."

If only Kerry could be so sure Grant would be released, but she wasn't. "I'm going back to the house to talk with Ford. Is there anything else I can get for you?"

"Only Grant's freedom."

Spoken like a woman in love, something that was more than obvious to Kerry, even if Anna Sheridan hadn't admitted it to herself, or to him. And as Kerry traveled back to deliver the news of Grant's alibi, she also recognized she had fallen in love with Grant Ashton's nephew.

During the drive back into the city, Ford tried to be optimistic, but even in light of Anna's revelations, he was too afraid to let himself believe. "It might not be enough," he muttered without taking his attention from the road.

"We'll have to wait and see. I personally think we have enough to get Grant cleared. Or at the very least, get him out of jail for the time being. We just have to keep hoping."

He reached across the console and took her hand. She had become his sanity, keeping him grounded yet providing an escape when he'd needed it most. "Thanks for everything. I owe you."

She lifted his hand and brushed a kiss across his knuckles. "You can pay me back when we get to the hotel."

Ford intended to do just that, with a long, hot session of lovemaking. He looked forward to holding her all night, waking up to her in the morning. Just thinking about that made him want to punch the accelerator and speed all the way back into the city. In deference to safety, he refrained.

After a few moments passed, Kerry pointed to a bend in the road that separated the highway from a gravel drive. "Turn right."

He shot her a look of confusion. "Why?"

"Because I want to see something."

Ford wanted to see her naked, and soon. But he couldn't refuse her anything right now, if ever. "Okay, but this better be good."

"It will be."

When he turned onto the narrow road, Kerry instructed him to pull over to one side. Once he had the vehicle parked, she hurried out of the car and rounded the hood, signaling him to follow. By the time Ford got out, she'd already crossed the street to stand on the other side.

As he approached her, she said, "It's beautiful, isn't it?" without turning around.

He had to admit that the rows of grapevines, turned gold by the light of the three-quarter moon, were pretty impressive, but not as impressive as Kerry.

Moving behind her, Ford wrapped his arms around her waist and pulled her against him. "You're beautiful."

She looked back at him and kissed his cheek before returning her attention to the panorama. "Does it look like this at midnight in Nebraska?"

"Yeah. Minus the vines, of course. Lots of corn, especially right before harvest. Abby and I used to play hide-and-seek in the stalks when we were kids. In fact, we hid from Grant or Buck on more than one occasion."

"That must have been wonderful."

At times Ford hadn't realized how much he'd taken for granted, until he'd seen the world through Kerry's eyes. "I had a good childhood." Even with an absent mother, who'd never been much of a mother at all.

"You know, mine wasn't so bad when my mom was alive. She used to take me on long walks and never told me I couldn't climb trees or swim in the creek. I miss being that carefree. I still miss her."

He was going to miss Kerry when he had to leave. Badly.

"I can't even imagine what it would be like not having Grant around."

"Then don't imagine it. Don't invite that into your life." She turned into his arms to face him. "Do you know what you need?"

"No, what do I need?"

She smoothed a hand over his chest. "A distraction."

He couldn't agree more. "Oh, yeah? What kind of distraction?"

"This kind." Clasping his nape with one hand, she bent his head to meet her lips and kissed him but good. A long, hot kiss that caused Ford's body to jolt to life.

She pulled away and smiled. "Did that help?"

"Some, but I could use a little more distracting."

"And I have the perfect way to do that."

Ford expected her to kiss him again, but instead she caught his hand and led him to the back of the SUV. After dropping his hand, she raised the rear door and climbed inside. Ford definitely enjoyed the view of her butt while she pulled a latch and pushed the rear seat forward.

Turning, she sat down at the edge of the cargo space, her long legs dangling, her skirt riding up her thighs, and patted the space beside her. "Come here and let me get your mind off your troubles."

Just thinking about what she might do had Ford close to losing his mind. Once he settled beside her, she slipped off her heels, tossed them behind her and then nudged him to his back.

"What exactly do you plan to do to distract me?" he asked although he was fairly sure he already knew the answer to that.

"Guess you'll just have to wait and see," she told him as she pulled the tails of his shirt from his jeans.

He sucked in a deep breath as she raised the polo until she had his abdomen exposed. "Now you really have my curiosity up."

Slowly she lowered his fly, keeping her gaze on his face as she traced the outline of his erection through his briefs. "I do believe your curiosity isn't the only thing that's up."

Quite an understatement. "You're definitely right about that."

Lowering her head, Kerry placed soft kisses right below his navel as she grasped his waistband. He gritted his teeth when she worked his slacks down his thighs. This kind of distraction could very well kill him. "Kerry, I…" He couldn't even form a coherent sentence.

After raising her head and nailing him with a sultry look, she reached up and pressed her fingertips against his mouth. "Hush and just let me do this."

"Someone might drive by," he muttered as she pushed his briefs down to join his slacks.

Surprisingly, she laughed while Ford didn't find a damn thing funny about the situation. Hot, but not humorous.

"We're on a rural stretch of road at a quarter past midnight," she said as she ran a slow fingertip down his length. "And if someone does happen to come by, too bad."

Too good, Ford thought when she enveloped him in her warm, sweet mouth. He twisted his hands in her hair to secure himself against the total sexual charge. With every pass of her tongue, every draw of her lips, he grew harder than stone, balanced on the brink of coming completely unwound.

As much as he enjoyed what she was doing, Ford didn't want it to end this way. He wanted to be inside her when he couldn't hold out any longer. He wanted her to take this trip with him.

Pulling her head up, he kissed her hard, kissed her quick, then said, "Do you still have that condom in your purse?"

She grinned. "Yes, sir, I sure do."

"Get it."

When she crawled forward and leaned between the front

seats, Ford couldn't resist lifting her skirt and forming his palm her between her thighs. As he'd predicted, she was hot and damp and ready for some action. And while she rummaged through her purse, he slipped his hand beneath the silk panties and touched her without mercy.

He heard her gasp before she declared, "Found it."

So had Ford, and he knew just what to do with it. Kerry went limp, her arms braced on the back of the passenger seat, her hips moving in sync with his fingers. He lifted her skirt, pressed his open mouth to her bottom and slipped a finger inside her. This time she moaned as he stroked her, inside and out, her breath riding out in an uneven tempo. She trembled as Ford quickened the pace, determined to rock her world the way she had rocked his. He didn't let up until he'd brought her to a climax than made her knees buckle.

She regarded him over her shoulder, her body still limp against the seat. "You are determined to drive me crazy."

"That's the plan."

"Plan or not, now it's my turn again." She scooted back and stretched out beside him, tore open the condom and did the honors herself. Ford realized they didn't have a lot of room but he was damn determined to make this work. While he was considering how he was going to get inside her without knocking himself out in the process, Kerry shoved his pants farther down, slinked out of her panties and then straddled his thighs. She guided him inside her, her hair flowing down in a golden veil around him. For a brief moment, he considered how this would look to anyone who happened by—his legs still partially out of the SUV, his pants down around his ankles and an incredible woman on top of him. Frankly, he didn't give a tinker's damn how it looked, not when Kerry took him on a reckless ride straight into oblivion.

He kept one hand on her breast and the other in motion between her legs as she moved in a slow rhythm up and down his shaft. "Don't hold back," he said in a harsh whisper, relinquishing all his control to her.

He saw understanding dawn in her expression before she resumed a wilder pace. He witnessed a total look of awe as the pleasure took over. He felt the pulse of her orgasm while he was seated deep inside her, and that nearly drove him over the edge completely. But he didn't want it to end now, even though his body was saying something different. Even though every muscle in his gut constricted with the effort to prolong the experience. Unable to fight any longer, he clasped her hips beneath the skirt and lifted his own hips to meet her with one final thrust. He shook from the strength of his own climax and automatically pulled her down against his racing heart.

When the world came back into focus as his breathing steadied and his body calmed, Ford felt the need to say something to Kerry, express his gratitude with words that wouldn't quite form. But what he was beginning to feel for her had only partially to do with appreciation of all that she had done in terms of lovemaking. She'd also disregarded his deception and given him a reason to hope for Grant's release. She'd decided to help him when most women would've probably sent him packing without a second glance. She'd inspired him more than any woman in his past.

Lifting her head, she smiled the sweetest smile and gave him the softest of kisses. "How do you feel now?"

He couldn't begin to tell her without sounding like a fool. "Like I could sprint all the way back into the city." Like he could fall for her completely.

She laughed quietly, a sound he could hear every day for the rest of his life and never tire of it. "I think it's probably best we drive so you don't wear yourself out, because there's plenty more distraction where that came from."

"You have my permission to distract me all night." And most likely she would distract him long after they parted ways.

# Eight

**K**erry had never before experienced going to sleep curled into a masculine body. She'd never known the pleasure of being awakened by a man's callused hands streaming up her body, or the joy of making love in the first light of dawn.

She'd also learned the benefits of showering with a gorgeous guy who had no qualms about engaging in some very devilish water play. Right now she sat on a vanity stool wearing the hotel robe while watching that same gorgeous guy rub a towel along his beautiful body—over his broad chest, across the flat plane of his belly and down his very masculine legs. He grinned as he worked his way back up his groin, totally uninhibited by the fact that she followed his movements.

After coming to her feet, she took the towel from him, wrapped it around his narrow hips and tucked it in below his navel. Holding her face in his palms, he kissed her lightly, then deeply until she considered yanking the towel away and stripping out of her robe.

Instead, she chose to end this little vacation from reality, knowing they still had a lot to do today that unfortunately didn't include making love for the remaining hours. Stepping back, she pointed behind her at the door. "I'm going to make some coffee and get the paper. Want me to bring you a cup?"

He caught her hand and pulled her back against him. "I want you naked again. I just plain want you."

She patted his bare chest, battling the urge to slide her hand down to find out exactly how much he wanted her. "You need to call Grant's attorney and Anna and arrange a time for them to meet us at the police station."

He released a rough sigh without releasing her. "Yeah, you're right. But I'm not holding out much hope Grant's alibi is going to hold any real weight."

"We don't have any choice. We have to try."

He studied her with a somber expression. "I know. But I'm worried we'll make matters worse, especially if they believe Grant is the one who blackmailed Spencer and Anna is somehow involved."

Kerry recognized Ford had a point. "I just have to believe that with all the investigative techniques at the police department's disposal, they're going to prove that theory wrong."

He pressed a kiss to her forehead. "You're going to have to believe enough for both of us."

"Don't give up, Ford. Somehow, someway, we will get your uncle out of jail."

Turning her around, he patted her bottom. "I need some coffee, woman."

She shot a stern glance over her shoulder as she headed toward the door. "Woman? Aren't we a regular little macho man this morning."

"Little?"

Kerry turned, hand braced on the door, to find Ford had removed the towel. Her gaze tracked downward to discover he was impressively aroused. "Okay. Big macho man."

He favored her with a dimpled grin. "That's better. Are you sure you don't want to come over here and sit on my lap for a while?"

"You are too much, Ford Ashton."

"And I can't get enough of you, Kerry Roarke."

Before she discarded good sense, Kerry walked out the door, chafing her terry-covered arms with her palms in reaction to the succession of heady chills. But beneath the bottom of the robe, she was extremely hot.

After setting the coffeemaker in action, she strode across the room, opened the door and bent to get the paper. The headline calling out from the page froze her solid:

Prosecution's Star Witness in Ashton Murder a Street Kid.

Straightening, she backed into the room and read the article with curiosity and major questions. She cataloged the facts—a homeless teenage street artist sketching passersby, identified only as Eddie, had seen Grant enter Ashton-Lattimer. At nine o'clock at night?

"Something interesting in there?"

Kerry faced Ford and held up the paper in both hands like a sign. "Yes, this."

Ford streaked a hand through his damp hair before taking the paper from her. He read silently for a time before turning his attention back to her. "They're hanging their case on a kid?"

"Obviously so, and I found several things odd about it. First, it says he was drawing when he saw Grant enter the building. It would have been dark by then. Second, street artists draw for money, so it doesn't make much sense for this kid to be down in the financial district when he could have been at the Wharf or The Haight hitting tourists up for a few bucks."

"Those are all good questions."

"Yes, and I intend to get some answers."

Ford rolled the paper in his fists. "How do you plan to do that?"

Kerry tightened the robe's sash and lifted her chin. "Easy. I'm going to find this Eddie and ask him. I know people who will know how to find him, and we will find him even if it takes all week."

"Even if we do find him, and that's a big 'if,' what makes you think he'll talk to you?"

"Because it takes a one-time street kid to know one. I have a few theories on what might have happened."

"Care to share them with me?"

"I will on the drive. First, you and I need to get dressed."

He approached her slowly and palmed her cheek. "You've been a godsend, Kerry. I don't know what I would've done without you these past few days. Thank you for everything."

She didn't know what she would do after he was gone from her life. Survive, the way she always had. But it wasn't going to be easy. Not in the least.

Laying her hand on his palm, she smiled to conceal her sudden sadness. "Don't thank me yet. This could be a dead end." Exactly like their relationship.

"It's a possibility," he said. "And for some reason, I have this gut feeling something good will come out of this with you in charge."

Kerry hoped it would, even the good they'd found together would be over soon if they were successful.

Ford has postponed calling Anna for the time being, at least until they could talk to the kid named Eddie. That proved to be a serious challenge. They'd been to The Haight, to Fisherman's Wharf then to a couple of shelters, with no luck.

Kerry refused to give up and by the time late afternoon had set in, they found themselves back at the Wharf.

Now Ford stood outside a small restaurant, waiting for Kerry to return from speaking with the owner. He leaned back against the red brick wall, arms folded across his chest, and prayed this time she might be successful.

"Eureka!"

Ford pushed off the wall to face Kerry who was coming toward him, a vibrant smile on her face. "You found him?"

She slipped her hand in the crook of his arm. "Her. We've been looking for a boy and she's a girl. I talked to J.D., the owner of the restaurant, and he says she left just a while ago after he gave her something to eat. He also said she's been skirting the press and the police, so she's been trying to lay low, but he thinks she probably headed over to where several homeless kids hang out. I imagine she's been hiding out there, with some help."

"Then she probably won't talk to us."

"She might talk to me, that's why I need to do this alone."

"But—"

"It's better this way, Ford. I know what her life is all about because I've lived it, and she could very well be wary of men. You're going to have to trust me on this."

Ford did trust her. He also realized how much he cared about her. So much it made him hurt. "Just promise me you're going to be careful."

She rose up on her toes and kissed him. "I will. First, I'm going to drop you off at the hotel and you can wait for me there."

"How are you going to find her? They didn't publish any kind of picture."

"J.D. described her to me. And I know where to look."

Ford took a moment to simply hold Kerry against him, probably tighter than he should. In adulthood, he'd learned to rely on himself and he'd liked it that way. Now he'd learned to rely on her for many things, and he'd discovered that hadn't been bad at all. In fact, it had been good. Damn good. Now he hoped she would come through for him once again.

Money definitely talked. Thanks to a kid who needed some quick cash, Kerry managed to locate the place where Eddie often hung out. A place all too familiar to a woman who had been there before.

Kerry spotted her sitting on a side-street curb, a sketch pad propped up against her black corduroy-covered knees, her long brown hair pulled back and secured at her nape, a dirty white baseball cap pulled low on her brow. The black T-shirt etched with Life Sucks was partially hidden by a frayed blue flannel shirt. Exactly how J.D. had described her.

Kerry moved cautiously toward the teen, calculating each step, planning each question. Stopping at a nearby light pole, she leaned a shoulder against it, her hands tucked away in the pockets of her navy blazer covering her jeans. She pretended to be hanging out, the misty evening fog beginning to set in as well as a definite chill.

Eddie seemed oblivious to her presence, her brows drawn down in concentration as she swept charcoal over the blank page, creating a picture of a field of flowers surrounding a child, the sun high in the imaginary sky.

"Wow, you're good," Kerry said.

Only then did the teen look up. "What?"

Kerry gestured toward the canvas. "The picture. You're very talented."

She flipped the page over to a blank one. "For ten bucks, I'll draw you."

"Okay." After dropping down on the curb beside her, Kerry retrieved a ten-dollar bill from her pocket and handed it to Eddie.

After shoving the money in her sneaker, Eddie asked, "You want a real picture or a caricature?"

"A caricature might be fun. Can you draw me sitting in a red Mustang convertible?"

"Yeah, I can do that. My mom owned a Mustang once." She opened a box containing assorted colored chalk and started to work.

"How long have you been living on the streets?" Kerry asked as she watched Eddie outline the car in accurate detail.

She continued to draw without looking up. "Who said I live on the streets?"

"Not too hard to figure out, considering where you are. I used to hang out here, too."

She gave Kerry a quick once-over. "You don't look like it."

Kerry folded the hem of her jacket when the memories assaulted her. "It was a while ago. How long have you been here?"

"About eight months."

"I lived on the streets for a year. I was sixteen. How old are you?"

"Fifteen." Eddie sent her a hopeful look. "But you got out."

"Yes. A woman helped me one night after I ended up in the hospital after an attack. I was lucky."

She shrugged. "It's not so bad. Better than home, that's for sure."

"I thought the same thing at the time. My stepfather kicked me out. At first I enjoyed the freedom, but it came with a price." Namely, the last vestiges of naïveté.

Eddie's strokes were so angry, Kerry thought she might break the red chalk in half. "My mom's boyfriend started messing with me. She just pretended not to see, so I took off."

Kerry's heart broke for her. "Where are you from, Eddie?"

Her hand froze and her gaze zipped from the page to Kerry. "How do you know my name?"

Kerry determined the time was right to tell her the truth, and take her chances. "Because I saw it in the newspaper. I've been looking for you all day."

Her eyes narrowed with suspicion. "Are you a cop or a reporter?"

"No, but I am a friend of the man you picked out in the lineup. I also know there's no way you could have seen him, because he wasn't there."

She lowered her gaze, but not before Kerry glimpsed her guilt. "I saw him."

"You couldn't have. He wasn't even in the city."

Eddie slapped the top back on the box and closed the sketch pad. "I've got to go now."

Kerry touched her arm to detain her. "Eddie, if someone threatened you and told you that you had to identify Grant Ashton, then you have to tell the truth."

She swiped a shaky hand over her cheek, leaving a streak of red in its wake. "Telling the truth gets you nowhere."

"It will in this case. Don't throw away your honor, Eddie. Even if that's all you have, it will see you through during the tough times."

Eddie raised her gaze, her eyes looking frightened and fatigued. "If you're right, and I'm not saying you are, what would they do to me if I change my story?"

Kerry's spirits elevated, knowing she was close to discovering the facts. "I don't know. You might have to spend some time in a juvenile facility."

"Maybe that wouldn't be so bad if I had some food and a bed. As long as they don't try to send me back home."

Some home, Kerry thought. "I'm sure they'll be lenient if you try to make it right before it's too late. Before they put the wrong man in jail. Especially if someone said they'd hurt you if you didn't lie."

Eddie wrapped her arms around her bent knees. "He didn't say he would hurt me. But he did give me money."

"He?"

"Some creepy guy. He came up to me when I was down at the Wharf and told me I could make a hundred bucks if I did what he said. At first I thought he wanted me to…you know."

How well Kerry knew. "Did he tell you his name?"

"No. He showed me a picture of that Grant and told me to go to the police and tell them I saw him going into the building around nine. They wanted to keep me there at the police station after I picked him out of the lineup, but I snuck out because I was afraid they'd call my mom. I've been hiding out ever since, but I figure they're going to find me soon."

"That's why you should go to them first and tell the real story. I'll be right there with you. Can you remember what this guy looked like?"

Eddie presented a sudden smile, easing some of the worry from her face and showcasing her youth. "I can go one better. I can draw him."

Ford stopped midpace when he heard the key slide into the lock and the door open, his heart jamming his throat. He turned to see Kerry enter the room, a bright smile on her face and optimism reflecting from her violet eyes.

Before he could reach her, she rushed him and hugged him hard. Ford pulled away first, only because he had to know what happened. "God, I was starting to worry about you when I couldn't find you."

Kerry's expression showed her confusion, understandably so. "Couldn't find me?"

"I followed behind the trolley until I saw you get off. I couldn't find a place to park and I lost sight of you, so I gave up and came back here."

"You were following me?"

"Yeah. I was worried sick the whole time. If something happened to you, I would never forgive myself. I was imagining all sorts of things."

She sent him a slight smile. "I promise, I'm okay. And you can't even imagine what happened, but it's all good. I found our star witness."

"Did you talk to her?"

"Yes, I did. She's waiting downstairs in the restaurant, consuming a cheeseburger. I have the waiter looking after her, in case she tries to slip out."

"What did she say?"

"You won't even believe it."

"Try me."

Kerry stepped out of his arms and withdrew a rolled-up piece of paper from her jacket pocket. "Do you know who this is?"

Ford studied the black-and-white sketch of a guy with thinning dark hair and beady eyes. "I've never seen him before." He handed the picture back. "Who is he?"

"I don't know, and neither does Eddie. But it seems he paid her to say she saw Grant going into the building the night Spencer was murdered. She sketched this picture of him."

"Then this means—"

"We should have enough evidence to clear your uncle."

Ford could only stare at Kerry for a long moment, speechless and in awe that she had somehow managed to help put all the pertinent pieces together. Had it not been for her, he doubted he would have been able to achieve this success. In fact he *knew* he could never have done this without Kerry Roarke—a woman who was as selfless as she was beautiful.

When he failed to speak, she frowned. "Why do you look so serious? This is great news. You should be shouting from the hotel rooftop."

Ford said the only thing he could think to say. "You are amazing." Amazing in more ways than he could begin to express.

She grinned. "All in a day's work. But if it makes you happy, I'll let you tell me how amazing I am, as soon as we get Eddie down to the police station."

"I plan on showing you later." All night long.

"That sounds extremely intriguing. But first you need to call Anna and see if she can meet us down at the station to give her statement."

As much as he wanted to show her how much he appreciated her right this instant, reality took hold. "I've already talked to her. She should be there in the next half hour. Caroline's driving her in. I'll call Edgar Kent on the way to the station."

"Then we should be on our way. The quicker we get out of here, the less time Grant spends in jail."

Kerry turned away but before she could open the door, Ford took her hand and tugged her back into his arms. He held on tight, never wanting to let her go. He didn't want to consider that their time together was almost over, barring any unforeseen glitches. He didn't want to think about not having her around. Not having her this close again. But he did think about it despite his concerns for Grant's well-being and his responsibility back home in Nebraska.

He gave her a quick kiss, then let her go. "Okay. I'm ready now." Ready to get back to the business of what he'd come here for—obtaining his uncle's freedom. But he wasn't ready to leave her just yet. Not until absolutely necessary.

"Looks like I won't be leaving for a while," Ford said as he pulled away from the police station.

Kerry experienced a solid bout of guilt that she wasn't at all displeased over that fact. "What exactly did the attorney tell you?"

"He said he'd file a motion for dismissal and that it could be Monday before they let him out."

"You'd think with everything they have now, they'd let him out tonight, not five days from now."

"Kent said it's a complicated process. Some crappy process, if you ask me. He also said he believes the D.A. still isn't convinced that Grant isn't behind this whole thing. Hopefully Kent can convince a judge there's enough doubt."

Reaching across the console, she took Ford's hand and rested it on her thigh. "It's going to happen, Ford. I can feel it in my bones."

He shot her a quick glance. "I hope you're right."

"I am. I just know it." She also knew that telling him good-bye would be the most difficult thing she'd done in years, and that time would come all too soon. Maybe even tonight.

Ford let go a long sigh. "That Eddie's a pretty sad case. It killed me to see her beg them not to send her back home."

"I know what you mean. That was tough. But unfortunately, she's only one of many lost kids in this city and throughout the country."

"What's going to happen to her?"

Kerry loved him for the true concern in his question. "The detective said she'd go to a halfway house for now. She promised she wouldn't put Eddie back into the home with the abusive boyfriend without some sort of investigation. However, it seems they can't even locate the mother, so it looks as if Eddie might eventually end up in foster care or a group home."

"How did she take that?"

"She seemed resigned to it all. I want to think that any place is better than the streets, but it's hard not knowing what will happen to her. I do plan to keep in touch with her."

"I have no doubt you will."

A few minutes later Ford turned into the hotel drive and

relinquished the SUV to the valet. Together they walked into the hotel, arms around waists, and didn't let each other go until they'd traveled up the elevator and arrived at the room. Only then did Ford drop his arms from around her to unlock the door. Yet they didn't take two steps inside the room before he had her backed up against the wall, kissing her, touching her, stealing her breath and her sanity in one fell swoop.

He left her lips to breeze his lips along her neck before working his way back to her ear. "We haven't had any dinner yet."

"I know," Kerry said while ruffling her fingers through his hair.

He ran his hands up the sides of her sweatshirt. "Anything in particular that you'd like?"

"Oh, I can think of one thing." She reached between them and ran a slow finger up the prominent ridge beneath his fly.

He caught her hand and held it there, pressing her farther back against the wall. "Do you want it now?"

"Yes."

He dropped his hand and cupped her between her legs. "Right here?"

"Yes."

"Then it's all yours."

He took her hand and led her to the hallway, but before they reached the bedroom, he backed her up against that wall. Off went her jacket, shirt, bra and jeans, leaving her wearing only her panties and panting as if she'd run a three-mile marathon. Ford was still dressed, not for long she hoped, but she stopped thinking altogether when he went to his knees and pulled her underwear down her legs, lifted each foot to remove it completely, then tossed it aside.

He pushed her legs apart with his palms and then kissed his way up the inside of her thighs, stroking his tongue over the territory. Kerry was virtually boneless, especially when he halted his journey to use his mouth on her in some terribly creative ways in a very intimate place. He suckled and nibbled and caressed with his lips and hands. She anchored herself by clutching his head, held on until she neared the edge of release. But before that happened, he kissed his way back up her trembling body, pausing to suckle her breasts. A slight groan of protest slipped out of her mouth before she could stop it.

"Don't worry," he whispered. "I plan to finish you in bed, while I'm inside you. I want to feel you climax."

Kerry wanted that too, but she also wanted to be daring and different. "Why the bed when we have a perfectly good wall?"

"You sure about that?" He sounded and looked concerned.

She traced the cleft in his chin with a fingertip then smoothed the worry from his brows. "Very sure. Unless it's too hard to manage."

His smile came into play slowly. "It's hard all right, but I can definitely manage it." He backed away and pointed to her. "Don't move."

As if she could really move at the moment. Then again, she might wilt onto the floor in a pool of need, a distinct possibility as she watched him walk toward the bedroom, stripping out of his jacket as he went. He came back a few moments later, wearing only a condom. He looked very proud. All of him.

Standing in front of her, Ford draped her arms around his neck, then pulled her legs around his waist and said, "Hang on."

She did, tightly, as he pushed inside her, going deeper than she ever dreamed possible. And when she immediately climaxed with the second thrust, her nails inadvertently dug into his shoulders with the strength of the release.

"Damn," he murmured. "This is almost too good."

Kerry couldn't describe how good she felt as he took her on a trip straight into the realm of a sexual place she'd never been before. She marveled at the strength of his legs as he bent to thrust inside her, his arms holding her and protecting her from the wall. Reveled in the power of his body and the sound of his ragged breathing. His skin grew damp with the effort and his eyes took on a hazy cast as he kept them locked with hers. She knew the moment he couldn't hold on any longer by the tautness in his jaw and the hiss that filtered out of his parted lips. He closed his eyes, tipped his forehead against hers and, with one last thrust, his body shuddered. Kerry continued to cling to Ford, holding him close to her body and her heart.

After lowering her legs, Ford kissed her thoroughly yet gently, then swooped her up and carried her into the bedroom. He set her on her feet and turned down the covers but not the lights before laying her back onto the crisp white sheets. He took a quick trip to the bathroom and when he came back he joined her on the bed and rolled her on top of him.

"I knew there was a wild woman residing somewhere beneath that sophisticated exterior," he said, his hands in motion on her bottom.

"And I knew beneath that innocent-farm-boy act I'd find a really wild man, too."

With a laugh, he flipped her over and hovered above her. "Have I told you how amazing you are?"

She tapped her chin with her fingertip. "I believe you did say that earlier. But it takes an amazing person to know an amazing person."

"I guess we'll both agree we're pretty amazing, at least together."

A wave of melancholy rode over Kerry, unwelcome after such a wonderful time. "I guess you won't be needing my services any longer now that we've solved the mystery."

He stared at her long and hard. "First of all, I don't like you using the word *services* like that's what this is all about. I didn't service you. I made love to you because I wanted to.

Second, I know it's selfish to ask, but I'm going to ask, anyway. I want you to stay with me."

"For how long?"

"Until Grant's out of jail."

Of course. He couldn't promise her more than that, and she'd known that all along. Still, it didn't hurt any less to know that she might be nothing more to him than a diversion, regardless of what he'd said. "Then you're asking me to hang around until Monday?"

"Yeah. But only if you want to."

Kerry wanted to, all right, even though she ran the risk of falling in so deep with him that she'd have to claw her way out. "I'll have to call Millie and tell her. It shouldn't be a problem since her niece planned to stay throughout the weekend."

"And you'll stay with me?"

Foolish or not, Kerry just couldn't pass up the chance. Besides, who knew what might happen in five days? Maybe she could somehow convince him that he couldn't live without her. And she would be certifiably stupid if she really believed that. But she'd be crazy not to try.

"Okay, I'll stay."

# Nine

**K**erry Roarke soon found herself caught up in an erotic world created by Ford Ashton. On Thursday morning they began their day by showering together, interrupted by the untimely arrival of housekeeping. Dressed in matching hotel robes, they allowed the maid to make up the room while they cuddled on the sofa in the living area, discreetly touching each other until they bordered on getting caught in some fairly illicit behavior. After the maid finished, Ford requested a surplus of extra towels, bade her goodbye, hung the privacy sign on the door and then made incredible love to Kerry on the sofa.

After that, they dispensed with clothes altogether, donning the robes again only if necessary, parting only when necessary, rarely more than a touch away. They watched the night set on the city and the sun rise over the bay, concealed by the sheer curtain covering the window while Ford stood behind her and made love to her. For the next few days they ordered in-room movies that they hardly watched and meals they rarely finished, consumed partial bottles of wine using most of the contents on each other's bodies.

Kerry learned it took Ford some recovery time between lovemaking sessions, but she also learned that, in regard to her own body, that wasn't always the case. And Ford had discovered that quickly, taking any opportunity he could to bring her to climax when she'd least expected it, using his hands or his mouth or both. She never viewed herself as being such a strongly sexual being before, but then she'd never let herself be that open and trusting with any man. Ever.

On Saturday evening Kerry convinced Ford to go out for dinner and they dressed for the first time in almost three days. She took him to Chinatown for a quick meal and a stroll among the weekly market set up at Portsmouth Park. But they only lasted a while among the chaos because they couldn't seem to keep their hands off each other. They openly kissed on the cable car during the return trip, and the minute they arrived back in the privacy of the hotel room, off went the clothes again, and they become sexually entangled on the living room floor.

By the time Sunday rolled around, Kerry had explored every inch of Ford's body, as he had hers. She'd willingly experimented with lovemaking in every way imaginable, and quite a few that she hadn't imagined. He'd always treated her with the greatest of care, even when their shared passion turned completely unrestrained.

She now knew the way he looked when he slept—tousled and beautiful and almost innocent—because she'd watched him on more than one occasion. She'd also awakened to him watching her with his sultry blue eyes, and invariably that would lead to more touches, more kisses, more incredible couplings.

During the times when they'd both been exhausted and sated, totally replete, they talked about Ford's fury over his mother's careless disregard; her anger over her stepfather's callousness. Both had decided to come to terms with their pasts and forgive, even if they couldn't forget. They'd also discussed all their likes and dislikes, faults and downfalls, goals and dreams. Yet when Monday morning arrived all too soon, they had yet to discuss one important thing—Ford's impending departure.

Kerry had also failed to tell Ford that she loved him, though she did with all her heart. In her life, she had never known a stronger truth. She had never known a more lovable man. But as they waited on the sofa for the call confirming Grant's release, Kerry didn't feel it was time to broach that subject. Even though she was wrapped securely in his arms, she sensed his tension and an underlying impatience. She understood that; he was ready to get on with his life. Without her.

His fingers idled on her arm as his deep voice drifted over her like a warm blanket when he asked, "What do you plan to do today?"

Nothing nearly as exciting as what they'd done the past few days. "First, I'm going to go home and change, visit with Millie, then go into the office. I'm going to have to work a little harder to catch up on my night courses since I missed a couple of classes last week."

"I'm sorry. I didn't even think about your school."

She whisked a kiss over his clean-shaven jaw, drawing in the scent of his cologne and taking it to memory. "I'm not sorry at all. I'd have to say I've learned quite a bit over the past few days."

He sent her a smile. "Yeah? What did you learn?"

That she'd fallen in love with him so deeply she didn't think she'd ever surface. "Mostly about myself. I had no idea I had that in me."

"And I had no idea that I had that much stamina. Must be the company I've been keeping."

"What do you plan to do when you get back home?"

"It's harvest time, and I have a few appointments with some feed suppliers. Just the same old thing I do every day."

"Plow the fields? Herd the cattle? Sun naked by the pool?"

"Something like that, except when I get naked, I'm going to be thinking of you."

There it was, the truth of the matter. She had been his distraction for days, but beyond that, he would think of her only in a sexual sense. "Have fun," she said without looking at him.

He pulled her face toward him and ran his thumb along her jaw. "I'd prefer to have the real thing instead of the fantasy."

"Guess you're just going to have to settle for the fantasy, huh?" She held her breath and waited, hoped for something, although what, she couldn't quite say. Maybe an invitation to come and visit, as if that would really happen.

He pressed his lips against her forehead. "I'm going miss you a helluva lot. I wish we didn't live so far apart."

Kerry wished that more than he would ever know. "But we do, and that's a problem. But you can e-mail me now and then, let me know how you're doing."

"I can do that now and then but we don't have good Internet access in Crawley. At least, not yet."

"Oh, well. It was just a suggestion."

"I could call you, if that's okay."

"Sure."

"Maybe you could come out to Nebraska for a couple of days in the spring."

Well, at least it was something, although Kerry realized not quite enough. "You know, Ford, I'm thinking it might be better if we just leave everything as it is. We've had a great time together, but having a long-distance relationship doesn't work."

"Have you ever had one?"

She'd never had a real relationship, period. "No, I haven't had one, but I don't think it's logical to assume that distance makes the heart grow fonder."

"Then you're saying after I leave, that's it? No phone calls. No visits."

Kerry was surprised by the anger in his tone. "Don't you agree that would be best?"

Taking his arm from around her, he leaned forward and studied the carpeted floor beneath his boots. "Maybe you're right. But I'm not going to forget you."

"And I'm not going to forget you, either."

Straightening, he pulled her to his side again. "I'm not going to fly out until tomorrow. Will you stay with me one more night?"

"I have a class. Remember?"

"Yeah, I remember. But it doesn't last all night, does it?"

"No, but I need to study."

Kerry needed to resist him, but when he kissed her again so completely, she wanted to forget everything but this moment. He was so tempting. So very, very tempting.

They parted, yet he still kept his arms around her, as it had been during the majority of their time together. "I'm glad we met, Kerry."

*And I love you, Ford.* "I feel the same, too. You're a very special man."

He hesitated a long moment, his heart seemingly calling out from his wonderful blue eyes. "What I'm trying to say is—"

When the phone rang, Ford bolted off the sofa and grabbed the receiver, leaving Kerry feeling incredibly bereft. He spoke in low tones, but when he ended the call with, "I'll be right down," she knew that the inevitable was upon them.

Kerry came to her feet, picked up her purse and bag and slipped both straps over her shoulder. "I guess that's the news you've been waiting for."

He shoved his hands into his pockets. "Yeah. Caroline's downstairs. She's going to give me a ride to the jail. Grant's being released as we speak."

"I'm so glad, Ford. I truly am."

"And none of this would be happening without your help."

Regardless of the fact her heart would surely break when he was gone, she didn't regret a minute of their time together. Didn't regret that she'd taken a chance on him after he'd deceived her, because now, more than ever, she knew his honor as well as she knew the touch of his hand, the sound of his voice, the feel of his body so close to hers. "I'm glad I was able to help. Please give your uncle my regards and tell him I'm very sorry for what he's suffered."

"Why don't you tell him yourself?"

"I really have to go, Ford. I need to get back to work." She needed to have a long cry.

He streaked a hand over the back of his neck. "Okay. I understand. But I'd like to at least talk to you before I go tomorrow."

"Sure. I'll give you my number. We can talk for a while tonight. Right now you better get downstairs. I'm sure Caroline's wondering where you are."

Fighting back a rush of tears, Kerry started for the door, but before she could grab the knob, Ford was there, pulling her around into his arms. He kissed her again, soundly, gently, movingly, until she felt as if she would never be able to react to another man in this way.

He released her and thumbed away a rogue tear that had fallen down her cheek despite her effort to stop it. "I'm going to miss you a lot."

"Me, too," she said, worried that if she said more, she might actually begin to sob. "I really need to get going."

"So do I. Will you at least walk down with me?"

"Sure."

He took her bag, took her hand and held on tightly to her even in the elevator. When they exited the car, the lobby was crowded with both businessmen and tourists checking out of the hotel. Kerry spotted Caroline first, standing alongside Anna Sheridan who was holding a precious little red-haired boy on her hip. And positioned beside Anna, the very tall, very handsome Grant Ashton.

Ford tightened his grip on Kerry's hand, then muttered, "I'll be damned."

"Looks like you have a nice surprise."

He stared at her momentarily, shock in his eyes and something else she couldn't quite name. After taking the bag from his shoulder, she smiled. "Don't just stand there. He's waiting for you."

"Come with me."

"This is your reunion. I'll be right here." At least for a few more moments.

Following another squeeze of her hand, Ford let her go, in every sense of the word. Kerry watched as he elbowed his way through the crowd and immediately embraced his uncle. Although she saw little resemblance between Ford and Grant Ashton, they both wore jeans and boots. Both emitted a confidence that was palpable even in the jam-packed lobby. Two men who stood above the crowd in every sense of the word.

The family gathered round then, his family, not hers. She didn't belong in this picture, would never be a part of his world. That realization sent her toward the revolving doors, but before she left she took one last look at the beautiful man with the unruly blond hair, the heartbreaker smile and the hypnotic blue eyes. The man with a heart of gold and hardworking, wonderful hands. The man who had totally captivated her from the moment they'd met.

Ford caught her gaze in that instant, and as if her heart protested the hasty departure before she'd revealed its secret, Kerry raised her hand in a wave and mouthed, "I love you."

Stunned by the spontaneous act, she rushed out the exit and hailed a nearby cab, leaving Ford Ashton behind, not knowing if he'd deciphered her declaration. Even if he had, would it make a difference? Probably not. But at least she could say she'd tried. The rest was up to him.

"You okay, bud?"

A long moment passed before Ford found the mental resources to join back in the conversation. He turned his gaze from the place Kerry had been to Grant. "Yeah. I'm fine."

He wasn't fine. Not in the least. Unless he'd imagined it, the woman who'd spent the better part of a week in his arms and his bed had just told him she loved him. And he didn't know what the hell to do now. He was torn between running after her to make sure his eyes hadn't deceived him, and remaining with the man who had devoted the better part of his life to raising him.

"I told Grant that Kerry Roarke was instrumental in gathering the evidence," Caroline said. "She's such a sweet, sweet girl, isn't she, Ford?"

Sweeter than any woman had a right to be. "Yeah. She's one in a million."

"And she wasn't tangled up with Spencer?" Grant asked.

"No. She was too good for that." When Ford realized his screwup, he sent Anna a look of apology. "I'm sorry. I didn't mean to insult your sister."

Anna smoothed a hand over the boy's head. "No apology

necessary. Alyssa made a huge mistake getting involved with him. Except, because of it, she had this little one. He'll never be a mistake."

Both Grant and Anna looked at the baby simultaneously before turning their gaze to each other. Ford saw something that looked like a lot more than just simple friendship. Right now he didn't have time to ponder anyone's love life other than his own.

"Ford, can I see you alone for a minute?" Grant asked.

Looking around the crowded room, Ford wasn't sure where they could go to have a private conversation. "Do you want to go back to my room?"

Grant pointed behind him. "Caroline and Anna need to get back to The Vines, so this will only take a minute. We can step outside." He regarded Caroline again. "If you'll excuse us, I have a couple of things to discuss with Ford."

Caroline waved a hand in dismissal. "Go ahead and take your time. We'll go into the restaurant and have some coffee."

"I'll make it quick," Grant said.

Ford was more than curious about the content of the impending conversation. He presumed Grant would want to know how things were going back at the farm, maybe how Abby was doing, too. When they stepped outside, Ford immediately scanned the sidewalk hoping to find Kerry. Obviously, she'd headed home to get ready for work. He planned to call her tonight, although he wasn't exactly sure what he would say to her.

Ford stayed in step with Grant as they strode down the sidewalk in silence, past a steady stream of tourists. After they went a block, he indicated the park where he'd sat with Kerry that first night ten days ago and told Grant, "Let's go over there."

They took the same bench in front of the same fountain,

and once they were settled in, Ford decided he'd had enough of the suspense. "What's on your mind, Grant?"

Grant leaned forward, hands clasped together between his parted knees. "How's Abby?"

"She was fine as soon as I called her and told her you'd be getting out soon."

"And the farm?"

"Russ and Buck have everything under control. We'll see for ourselves when we get back. By the way, I made your reservation last night, so we're set to go tomorrow."

"Cancel it."

"What?"

"I'm not leaving California yet."

"Why the hell not?"

"Because the D.A. strongly suggested I stick around until they find the murderer. I think he still assumes I had something to do with it."

After all they'd done, Grant was still under suspicion. That didn't sit well with Ford at all. "Where are you going to stay?"

"At The Vines like I was before. Caroline asked me to, and I agreed."

Ford strongly suspected that Anna had something to do with that decision, too. "How long do you intend to stay gone?"

"Until my name is cleared and I find out exactly who killed Spencer."

"That could take years, if ever."

"Then I'll be here that long."

Ford wanted to knock some sense into his uncle, but even a left hook to the jaw wouldn't cure him of his stubborn streak. Not that he would ever actually punch Grant. Not if he wanted to live to tell about it. "Okay. Have it your way. Abby's going to be pissed off if you're not there when the babies are born."

"Maybe we'll get lucky and I'll be home by then."

A span of silence passed before Ford asked, "Anything else you want to talk about?" He figured at some point in time, Grant might want to discuss his jail experience, although he wasn't one to be that open with his feelings. But then, neither was Ford.

"I just wanted to say thanks. You've done me proud, as always."

"Again, I only had a small hand in it. If Kerry Roarke hadn't helped me, I doubt we'd be sitting here together now."

"You like her," Grant said in a simple statement of fact, not a question.

"Yeah."

"Did you spend a lot of time with her?"

Not nearly enough. "Every day since I've been here."

Without straightening, Grant glanced back at him. "Every night, too?"

Ford started to lie but realized Grant would see right through him, as he always had. "For the most part, yeah. Are you going to lecture me about it?"

"You're a grown man, Ford. I'm not going to tell you how to run your life even if you are in love."

In love? "I didn't say that." He did sound way too defensive.

Finally Grant leaned back against the bench. "You don't have to say it. I saw you looking at her when she left, and I saw what she said to you. It's pretty damn obvious to me how you two feel about each other."

"I admit, I do care about her. A hell of a lot more than she realizes."

"Did you tell her that?"

He'd wanted to that morning, but the timing just hadn't been right. Either that, or he'd been too afraid of his own feelings, a more logical explanation. "No, I didn't tell her."

"Then I suggest you go find her and talk this out. What I said to you in that letter about settling down, I meant it. Don't let the right woman pass you by."

"What exactly are you suggesting I do?"

"Ask her to come back with you."

"She won't do it."

"She might."

"She wouldn't stay."

Grant's jaw tightened, and Ford braced for a verbal assault. "Dammit, Ford, not every woman is your mother. If this Kerry feels the same way about you as you do about her, she might be willing to make your home her home."

"She has a home here, Grant."

"Well just maybe she might believe her home's with you. If not now, eventually. All you can do is try. Otherwise you're going to end up like me, in the prime of your life without a good woman to share in it."

"You're only forty-three, Grant, not ninety. One of these days you're going to find the right woman."

Grant looked cynical. "If you say so."

Ford started to ask Grant if he might have found that woman in Anna Sheridan but thought better of it. Grant could dish it out, but he sometimes couldn't take it. The last thing Ford wanted was to get into a heated discussion about relationships. But he was beginning to see the wisdom in his uncle's words.

As soon as he saw Grant off, he would go back to the hotel room and think about it. He had until tonight to decide whether it would be best to return home never knowing the possibilities, or to shore up some courage and tell Kerry exactly how he felt about her. He would have to weigh the risk of asking her to come back to Nebraska with him and face her rejection. Worse, she might agree and then eventually, leave him, too.

* * *

"I was beginning to wonder if you'd run off with your fellow, my dear."

With only a cursory glance at Millie, Kerry started up the staircase to her room. "I'm here, and I'm running late. I need to get dressed and get back to work."

"Kerry Ann, I need to speak with you about something now."

With one hand braced on the banister, Kerry faced Millie and sighed. "Can it wait? We can have a nice dinner together tonight and catch up."

"I would prefer not to wait. I wouldn't ask if this were not of the utmost importance."

Resigned to the fact her mentor wasn't going to give up, Kerry trudged down the three steps she'd taken and followed Millie into the kitchen. They sat across from each other at the oak dinette in the usual places, Millie's prim hands folded before her, Kerry's white-knuckling the edge of the table.

"Did Sandra leave?" Kerry asked.

"Yes, dear. Early this morning, as soon as we finalized our plans."

"Plans?"

Millie looked disturbed. Very disturbed. "She has asked me to come live with her, and I've agreed."

Kerry swallowed around her shock. "When did you decide to do this?"

"While you were with your young man."

Millie was mistaken. Ford wasn't hers at all. "What about the house?"

"I'm afraid I'll have to sell it."

And Kerry had thought she couldn't be more stunned. Wrong. "But it's been in your family for years. It's your home."

"A home that I have mortgaged to the hilt. My pension will no longer cover the payments, much less the upkeep."

"I can help out more."

Millie reached out and pulled Kerry's hand into hers. "My angel, your salary can't begin to cover my debts. I admit that I have squandered my fortune, but I did so with the best of intentions."

She'd given most of it away, Kerry realized. To foundations, to the needy, to her. "You don't have anything at all left?"

"Only a small amount of savings and the roadster, as well as all the furnishings. And you are welcome to anything here that you wish."

Great. She would have furnishings, but no house. No home. "I couldn't do that, Millie. Besides, I'm sure Sandra would like to have some of your things."

Millie waved her free hand. "Posh. Sandra has her own furnishings. And she will never cherish my things the way you will."

Kerry felt as if Millie had told her she was about to pass on to the great unknown. "You've always told me you've never gotten along that well with your niece. How are you going to live with her?"

"As best I can. I have no choice."

Kerry bit her bottom lip, hard, to stop the threat of tears. "I wish there was something I could do."

Millie squeezed her hand. "My dear, you have done so much already. You have been the best companion. The best daughter a woman could ever hope for. I only wish…" Her gaze drifted away.

"You wish what?"

"I wish that I wasn't forced to put you out in the street." She leveled her sad eyes on Kerry. "Perhaps Ford will be asking you to go with him?"

The hopefulness in Millie's voice only added to Kerry's despair. "I'm afraid that's not going to happen. He's leaving tomorrow. He has a life somewhere else, not with me."

"But you wish that weren't so, don't you?"

This time Kerry looked away. "I'm a realist, Millie. I had a wonderful time with Ford, but I knew all along it couldn't last." And though she owned that knowledge, she still didn't hurt any less.

"You say he isn't leaving until tomorrow?"

"That's right."

"Then perhaps between now and tomorrow he will have a change of heart."

"That's not likely, Millie. Again, we had a nice time together, but it was less than two weeks. You can't make a decision like that in such a short time."

"My second husband and I only knew each other five days and we married on the sixth. Anything is possible."

Kerry wanted to believe as strongly in miracles, the way Millie always had. But she had yet to see anything that qualified, except for the miracle of making love with Ford. Tugging her hand from Millie's grasp, she came to her feet and offered a smile. "You go on believing that, but it's time for me to go back to the real world. And that means going back to work."

"Yes, dear. You do that. In the meantime, I have errands to run and a bridge game tonight, so you might return from your class before I get home. Do you want me to drop you at work?"

"No, thanks. I'll probably walk." Kerry needed to walk off her melancholy. In fact, she probably should run in hopes of escaping thoughts of Ford Ashton. But that would require a lengthy marathon and even then she couldn't guarantee she would forget him. Not today. Not tomorrow. Not ever.

# Ten

**H**ow could he forget her when everywhere he looked she was there? Standing by the window. Lounging on the sofa. Lying in his arms.

Ford paced the hotel room, restless with each hour that passed. He'd picked up the phone twice to call her at work, stared at the receiver, started to dial, then hung up. He didn't know what to say or what to do. He hated the thought of leaving without at least a proper goodbye, another kiss. Maybe even another round of lovemaking. But it wouldn't be fair to ask her to be in his bed if he couldn't offer her more than that.

A sharp rap came at the door, sounding like wood against metal. Ford started not to answer, but the prospect of Kerry standing on the other side sent him across the room in a rush. But he didn't discover Kerry on the threshold. He did find Kerry's landlady leaning both hands on her cane, a look of disapproval on her face made worse by her severe scowl.

"I have a bone to pick with you, young man."

Ford had no doubt she did, considering she looked like she could beat him about the face and head with her walking stick. "Come in, Mrs. Vandiver."

She hobbled past him and before he even had the door closed, she spun on him. "I have a question to ask you, and I want you to think about it before you answer."

Ford slid his hands into his jeans pocket. "Okay. Shoot."

"Do you realize what you'll be losing if you let Kerry Ann go?"

"Yeah, I do."

Ford was taken aback by the ease of the admission, and so was Millie, apparently, when she said, "You do?" in an awed tone.

"She's a special woman," he said. "Probably the best woman I've ever met."

Millie pointed her cane at him like a weapon. "Then why in heaven's name would you take off without her?"

"Because I don't think she'd consider leaving you. And even if she did, I'm not sure she'd be happy in Nebraska. She's told me several times San Francisco's her home."

Millie clucked her tongue. "My dear, Kerry has never really had a home. True, she has shared my house, but it's never been her own in the way most of us know. And now I'm afraid she won't have that any longer."

"You're going to put her out?"

"In a way, yes. And I hate that more than anything I've hated in my lifetime."

The woman was making no sense to Ford. "Then why would you do it?"

"Because I have no recourse but to move in with my niece. For all intents and purposes, I am broke."

She was broke, and Kerry would be homeless again. No one should have to suffer that once in a lifetime, much less twice. Especially not the woman he loved.

*The woman he loved.*

There it was, the cold, hard truth. A truth he was more than willing to accept.

"When are you going to have to move?" he asked, like that really mattered.

"By the end of the month. Kerry can remain until the house sells, but after that she'll have to find a new place to reside." Her thin lips curled up into a smile that revealed what Ford suspected was a fine set of dentures. "I hear Nebraska is a very nice place to live."

Ford had rarely heard anyone say that; at least, not any woman he'd known before. "Are you telling me I should ask her to come live with me?"

"Yes, but only if you love her. Only if you're willing to give all of yourself to her and pledge to make her happy. And only if you promise me you will bring her and your children to visit me often."

Children. He'd never let himself consider having any. But he'd want that with Kerry. Want to see her belly swollen like Abby's. Want to make love to her every night of his life. But would she want that, too?

Ford rubbed a hand over his neck and studied the floor. "I'm not sure she'll agree."

"Have you asked her?"

"No."

"Do you love her?"

He raised his gaze so Millie could see the sincerity in his eyes. "Yes."

"How much?"

More than he realized. More than he loved his freedom from commitment. "Enough to ask her to marry me, as insane as that sounds."

Millie tossed back her head and laughed. "Oh, my dear, that's not insanity. That's the voice of love speaking. And you'll do well to listen to it."

Driven by a sudden sense of purpose, Ford snatched the keys to the rental off the table and pocketed them. "Where is she now?"

"I imagine she's at home, studying. I'm certain she will enjoy your company. Myself, I have a card game that could go well into the night, especially if I happen to find myself on a winning streak for a change."

The woman was a real piece of work. "You bet on bridge?"

Taking Ford by surprise, Millie moved to his side and linked her arm in his. "Truthfully, my friends and I prefer a good game of penny poker. Much more interesting, don't you agree?"

He grinned. "Yeah, I guess so."

"Now you may escort me to my car, and then you will see to my charge."

"Sounds like a plan."

Once they reached the hotel door, Millie faced him again. "I didn't trust you when I first met you because I sensed you were hiding something. And now I know what that something is."

Ford frowned. "What do you think I've been hiding?"

"Your heart. But now that it's in the open, you must give it all to Kerry."

He patted her hand resting in the bend of his arm. "I already have, Millie."

Broken hearts sucked as much as calculating interest rates. Kerry sat in the middle of the bed she'd slept in for the past

ten years, a book sprawled in her lap, plagued with the beginnings of a mild headache and a heartache the size of the home
she would soon be forced to leave.

She couldn't concentrate on the text before her, even knowing she was behind in her studies. Her goal to obtain her real
estate license wasn't as pressing as facing the prospect of
never seeing Ford Ashton again, or hearing his voice one last
time. He hadn't bothered to call, even though she'd stared at
the bedside phone several times for the past two hours, as if
she could will it to happen. But she couldn't force him into
doing something he didn't want to do, and obviously her little spontaneous declaration had meant nothing to him. Either
that, or it had prompted him to catch a plane tonight instead
of tomorrow.

When she heard the bedroom door creak open, Kerry didn't
bother to look up. No doubt Millie had opted to leave her
bridge game early and would now embark on a session of
"let's grill Kerry about her love life" for Lord only knew how
long. She was simply too tired to deal with it.

"Lose all your pennies?" she asked, pretending to peruse
the page.

"Nope. Just my mind."

Kerry's whole body went rigid at the sound of the deep,
endearing voice. Her entire heart took a tumble at the same
time. Slowly she lifted her eyes to find him standing there, all
six-foot-plus of potent male wearing washed-out jeans that
showcased his long legs and a starched pale-blue shirt that
contrasted with his golden skin and highlighted his lumines-
cent eyes.

When she failed to speak, he asked, "Am I interrupting
something?"

Only her ability to take in a decent draft of air. "No. I'm

just trying to catch up on some things." Trying not to launch herself off the bed and into his solid arms.

"Mind if I sit down and talk to you for a minute?"

She would mind if he didn't. "Sure." After tossing the book aside, she patted the space beside her. "Take a load off."

He crossed the room with the same confidence she'd noticed the first time she'd seen him. But his eyes looked much less self-assured as he slid onto the edge of the mattress.

"I'm surprised Millie sent you up here without insisting on serving as a chaperone," she said, keeping her tone light.

"Millie's not here."

"Then how did you get in?"

"With Millie's key."

None of this was making any sense to Kerry. "Excuse me?"

He shifted slightly. "Millie paid me a visit today at the hotel. We had a talk."

So that's why he was here, at Millie's insistence. That made Kerry's heart even heavier. "I'm sure that was interesting."

"You could say that. She told me she was going to move."

Kerry sighed. "I was afraid of that. If you're worried about me, I'll be okay."

"I'm sure you will. Have you thought about where you might go?"

She shrugged. "I can't stay in this area because I can't afford it. I'm sure I'll find an apartment somewhere."

"I know of a place that might interest you."

"Where?"

"It's a house. Three bedrooms, three baths—"

"I can't afford anything like that."

"Yes, you can."

"Trust me, I can't."

His expression remained unreadable. "Just hear me out, okay?"

Kerry wasn't quite comprehending any of this scenario. "Okay. First of all, where exactly is this place?"

"It's kind of in the middle of nowhere, surrounded by a lot of land. The only disadvantage is you have to drive a ways to find a mall. Entertainment's hard to come by, but the people are simple and basically good."

"This doesn't sound like California."

"It isn't in California."

A little glimmer of hope began to shine through Kerry's confusion. "Then where is it?"

"In Nebraska. I know the owner personally, and so do you. Better than any woman has ever known him."

Although things were beginning to make sense, Kerry was still hard-pressed to let herself believe. "Who is he?"

Ford took her hands into his and held them against his heart. "A man who loves you more than he's ever loved anyone or anything in his life."

Tears stung the backs of her eyes. "Ford, I don't understand what you're saying."

"You know exactly what I'm saying, even if I'm not saying it that well. I love you, Kerry, and I want you to come back to Nebraska with me. As my wife."

She felt faint and giddy, but all she could do was stare at him in disbelief. "Are you serious?"

"As serious as I've ever been about anything in my life. But I have to know two things. First, if what I saw you say to me is true—that you love me. And if you'll even consider marrying me, if not now, then whenever you're ready."

She raised his hands to her lips and kissed them. "Yes, I love you. I wanted to tell you that last night, out loud, and I almost did, but then…" She smiled. "You know the rest."

He inched off the bed and pulled her up into his arms.

"Yeah, I know the rest. I've been thinking about it all day. Thinking about you."

"Me, too," she said, followed by a rogue sob. "I can't believe this is happening. And I can't believe I'm seriously considering your offer."

"You are?"

"Unless you're only doing this because you're worried I'm going to end up back on the streets."

He swept a warm kiss across her forehead. "No, I'm worried you'll end up with another man, and I couldn't stand the thought of that happening. In fact, I can't stand the thought of being without you even a day from here on out. So?"

She couldn't help teasing him just a little. "So what?"

"Are you going to marry me?"

"Well, I do have school to consider. I'll be finished by the end of the month, and I've worked so hard to get my license, I don't want to blow it now."

"You can sell land in Nebraska. We have more than our share there. I'll have to go back to the farm and check on things, but I'll be back for you, as long as I know you'll be waiting for me."

Waiting with all the love in her heart. "Promise?"

He studied her face and touched her cheek. "Sweetheart, nothing could keep me away from you, you can count on that."

Kerry knew she could count on that, and him. But now it was time to broach a more serious issue. "There is another consideration. Millie. I know she'll be taken care of, but I hate to think I'll never see her again."

"You'll see her. I promised I'd bring you and our kids back for visits."

Her smile came full force. "Kids, huh?"

He grinned. "Yeah. I never thought I'd have any, but I want that now, as long as it's with you."

"I want that, too." More than she realized until this point. "I think we'll be good at it."

He whisked a kiss over her lips. "I'm sure we will, considering how good we are at the baby-making process."

"You're right about that." She pressed against him. "Maybe we should get in a little practice."

"Not until you tell me yes."

She frowned at him, mock serious. "You're going to refuse to have your way with me until I officially agree to marry you?"

"Yeah, I am."

"Well then, I guess I'll have to marry you."

He picked her up off her feet, swung her around, then set her back down to deliver a kiss so full of emotion and passion, Kerry's head whirled from the effects. Once they parted, he told her, "I have another idea."

"You want to make love on the floor?"

"Not a bad suggestion, but this has to do with Millie."

She released the first button on his shirt. "Millie will have to get her own man."

He caught her hand and stilled it against his chest. "I've been thinking about her situation and I've decided I'll pay off her mortgage so she can live out the rest of her days right here. No one should ever have to leave their home."

Oh, how she loved him in that moment. "She's got a lot of pride and because of that, I'm not sure she'll agree. Plus, she's not getting any younger. She needs someone to stay with her."

"I thought about that, too. I know a lost and lonely teenager who might fit the bill."

Kerry was confused again until the light of comprehension suddenly snapped on. "You mean Eddie?"

"Yeah. Do you think Millie would agree to that?"

"I know she would. And I would find comfort knowing that she'll have someone to replace me."

"You're wrong about that, Kerry. No one could ever replace you. You can take my word on that."

This time Kerry kissed him, putting all of her love into the gesture. "You're a remarkable man. Did you know that, Ford Ashton?"

"We're remarkable together. So when are you going to marry me?"

"As soon as we find a suitable place to do it."

His gaze shot to the bed and without warning, he grabbed the hem of her top and tugged it over her head. "I believe right here will do fine."

She released the rest of the buttons on his shirt, grinning all the while. "I meant a suitable place to have a wedding."

He dispensed with his shirt and kicked out of his jeans and briefs, then said, "You just happen to be in luck."

"Oh boy, am I," she said as she noticed the extent of his arousal.

He went to work on her clothes, leaving her naked and needy in record time. After he took her down onto the bed, he told her, "I was talking about the wedding."

Kerry frankly wasn't sure she could talk at all when Ford sent his hands over her body. "What about the wedding?"

"I just happen to know this special place."

"You most certainly do," she murmured as he caressed her with his gifted hands, loved her with his tender mouth. All talk of the wedding ceased, but Kerry wasn't that concerned about the location or the time. Her only concern was Ford filling her completely, both heart and soul as he told her again and again that he loved her, while he made sweet love to her. She didn't care where they married, or when, as long as they spent the rest of their days together suspended in this lovely state of bliss.

Ford had taken Caroline up on her offer to hold the ceremony at The Vines, the one he'd scoffed at less than a month ago. They'd settled on a spot by the small lake, keeping the event simple, with only a select few family members in attendance. Abby had gladly agreed to serve as Kerry's attendant, and Grant had proudly filled in as best man. The ceremony had been brief but to the point, that point being that he and Kerry had vowed to be together for life. A life he'd once believed he would spend alone. Not anymore.

An all-around perfect day for a wedding, according to the guests. But Ford decided absolute perfection now stood only a few feet away, wearing the satin dress she'd borrowed from his sister, her blond hair burnished by the setting sun, the lake serving as a great backdrop for her beauty. She was chatting with Abby and Millie, Eddie standing nearby, looking and acting completely different from the sad, circumspect girl who'd almost sent his uncle to jail. According to Kerry, Millie was a master at working wonders with lost souls. From the looks of this version of one of those lost souls, he'd have to agree.

Ford was only mildly aware of Grant's and Russ's conversation involving cattle and commodities coming from beside him. The only thing that held his interest at the moment was Kerry Roarke Ashton. He'd arrived back in California two days before and had barely had time alone with her, much less made love to her. They'd communicated for two weeks by phone and, granted, some of those conversations had turned sexy enough to sear a few cornstalks. But it hadn't been the same as the real thing, and the prospect of the real thing had him ready to get out of there and get on with the honeymoon. He intended to do just that real soon.

"I need to talk to you and Abby for a few minutes, Ford. It's important."

Ford turned his attention to Grant and immediately noted his serious expression. "What about?"

"I'll tell you as soon as you get your sister over here."

"Do you want me to give you some privacy?" Russ asked.

Grant shook his head. "No. You need to hear this, too. So does Kerry."

Ford couldn't begin to guess what this was all about, but he worried it could be something that might ruin the day and his good mood. "I'll call them over."

Turning back to Kerry, he noticed Millie and Eddie had left and in their place stood Caroline's daughter, Mercedes. But she was only there for a time before a look of alarm crossed her face and she rushed away toward the house.

Ford whistled and gestured at Kerry. Abby followed her over and while they walked, he heard Kerry ask, "What do you think's wrong with her?"

"I'm guessing nothing that won't be cured in a few months," Abby muttered.

Ford suspected they were talking about Mercedes, and although he was somewhat curious, he was more concerned with Grant's sullen mood. Still, he couldn't help teasing his sister a little, for old-time's sake.

"Hey, Abigail, stick out your arms so I can tell if you're walking or rolling."

"Shut up, Ford, or I'll tell your wife all your dirty little secrets." She said it with a smile while rubbing her distended belly, prompting Ford to imagine what it would be like to see Kerry pregnant with his child. He figured he'd look as proud as Russ, who wrapped his arm around Abby and pulled her close to his side.

Ford did the same with Kerry, finding comfort in her presence, knowing Grant was about to lay some serious stuff on them. What, he couldn't say. But he knew his uncle well enough to know that what Grant was about to tell them would qualify as anything but light conversation.

"Now that you're all here," Grant began, "I have something important I need to say. I wasn't sure now was the time or place, but since I'm not going to be home for a while, I decided now is as good a time as any."

Abby looked as concerned as Ford felt. "You're scaring me, Grant."

Grant toed the grass beneath his boot. "I don't mean to scare you. In fact, I'm hoping you'll think this is good news, because it is."

Ford wondered if maybe he was about to announce his own engagement to Anna Sheridan, who was sequestered away with the rest of the guests beneath the white tent set up for the reception. But that didn't make sense. If Anna was involved, most likely she would be there.

"This is about Buck," Grant continued. "And his relationship with you."

Buck? Ford couldn't imagine what the ranch foreman had to do with this. "Is he sick?"

"No, nothing like that. He wanted to tell you himself, but I convinced him it might be better coming from me."

"Just spill it, Grant," Ford said.

"I will, but you two have to promise to listen with an open mind."

Abby shot a meaningful glance at Ford. "We can do that."

Grant let go a rough sigh. "Back when your mother and I were teenagers, Buck came to work for your great-grandparents. During that time, Grace was wild as a March hare and your grandmother had a hard time keeping her under control. But she tried as best she could, making sure Grace didn't leave the farm, at least not without Buck. As it turned out, she and Buck became involved."

Ford feared he knew where this might be leading, but his mind rejected that notion until Grant said, "And that's when Grace became pregnant with you, Ford."

He spoke around his shock. "Then you're telling me—"

"That Buck is your dad. He's Abby's dad, too."

Abby looked at Ford with disbelief. "Ford and I aren't half siblings?"

"No. Buck fathered you both."

Ford glanced at Kerry, who stood by silently, taking it all in, before regarding Grant again. "Why in God's name didn't you tell us before now?"

"Because I didn't know until now," Grant said. "Buck and I had a long talk last night and that's when he admitted it to me, although I guess I always wondered in a way. And before you start passing judgment on him, you have to understand why he didn't come forward. He loved your mother, but she told him he wasn't good enough for her. He was illiterate until Abby taught him to read. But he always believed Grace was right and that you two were better off not knowing."

"How could we be better off not knowing?" Abby said, echoing Ford's thoughts. "And why did he decide we needed to know now?"

"Because of the babies. He figured you'd want to know any medical history that he could provide. And because he loves both of you a lot. That's why he stuck around all those years, watching you grow and making sure you were treated well."

Ford had to admit that Buck had always been there for him,

but did that excuse him from withholding such an important fact? "This is a lot to handle, Grant."

Grant forked a hand through his hair. "I know. But you'll both handle it in time. When you get back to the farm, I expect you to talk with him, let him explain his motivation for keeping this a secret. He also said that he'd be willing to take a paternity test to prove it."

"That won't be necessary." And it wasn't, as far as Ford was concerned. Abby had Buck's hair color, and he had his smile. He just couldn't believe he hadn't seen it before now, but he had no real reason to see it. "After all this time, I'm not sure it really matters, Grant."

Grant leveled a serious stare on him. "It does matter. Buck's always been family, and now it's official. I expect you to treat him as you always have because he's done a lot for you."

"And so have you, Grant," Abby said. "This doesn't change the way we feel about you. You've been a father to us, too. I just want you to know that."

"I do know that." Grant glanced at the tent. "Now if you'll excuse me, I want to visit with a few of the guests." With that he walked away, leaving Abby and Ford staring at each other in stunned silence.

"Why don't we take a walk?" The first words Kerry had uttered since the revelations had begun.

"We'll do the same," Russ said, taking Abby by the arm and guiding her away.

Now more than ever Ford was glad to have Kerry by his side, holding his hand tightly in hers as they walked along the lake's edge in the opposite direction of the festivities.

After they'd put a good distance between themselves and the tent, Abby stopped and faced him. She laid a gentle palm on his jaw. "Are you okay?"

"I'm not sure." And he wasn't. Right now he felt like he was on information overload.

"This is a good thing, Ford," she said. "I never knew my real father, and the one that I did know didn't have a clue how to be a good parent. You've been lucky enough to have two great dads."

"And I've spent years trying to fill in that blank space of my heritage, and the answers were right under my nose. I can't believe Buck's been lying all along. I thought I knew him better than that."

"You heard Grant. He had his reasons. Good ones."

"His reasons just might not be good enough."

Kerry took both his hands into hers and gave them a squeeze. "Ford, I want you to think about this. When we met, you had your reasons for lying to me, and they involved protecting Grant. Maybe Buck thought he was protecting you."

"From what?"

"From what he viewed as shame. I don't know him, but I wouldn't be surprised if that's what drove him. When you have someone tell you often you're not good enough, you start to believe it. My stepdad had me convinced of that very thing. Had it not been for Millie, I still might believe it."

Everything she said made perfect sense, but the knowledge was still a lot for Ford to swallow. "I understand that, but it feels like such a damn big betrayal."

She surveyed his eyes for a long moment. "Do you love him, Ford?"

"Yeah, I do."

"Will knowing what you know now really change that? After all, once I finally understood you and your motives for deceiving me, I think that's part of why I fell in love with you, as crazy as that sounds. You were willing do anything for someone you loved. That's why I forgave you. And I hope you'll find it in your heart to forgive Buck."

Right now Ford would move every mountain in the state for her. "And I still can't believe how damn lucky I am to have found you."

"We're both lucky."

She circled her arms around his waist, he framed her sweet face in his palms and, regardless they were out in the open, he kissed his wife with all the gratitude, all the love for her he was feeling at that moment.

Once they parted, Kerry gave him a special smile, then one he knew very well. "You know, I'm really, really ready to get out of this dress and these heels."

"And I'm really, really ready to help you do that. But I think we're going to have to find a better place to do that first." He checked his watch and noted the lateness in the hour. "We have a plane to catch in less than three hours, so I'm thinking that's a great excuse to leave."

"True. How long will it take to get back to Nebraska?"

"With the layover in Denver, about four and a half hours. Then we have another few hours' drive to Crawley. Which means we won't be there until dawn."

"That's quite a long trip. You don't happen to be a member of the Mile-High Club, do you?"

He grinned. "Nope, but I'm open to getting a membership. Or to be on the safe side, we could stay in Denver for a few days and have a real honeymoon. We don't have to be back to the farm that fast."

She pressed her lips against his cheek then pulled back. "As much as I want to make love with you, I have my reasons for wanting to get to the farm as fast as possible."

"Oh, yeah? What reasons?"

"In my life, I've only wanted two things. Someone to love

who loved me back, unconditionally. And a home of my own. I have that someone in you, and now I can't wait to see the home where I plan to spend the rest of my life loving you well and raising our children. Can you understand that?"

Ford understood that completely. She'd never had a place where she'd belonged, and what she probably didn't realize was how firmly embedded she was in his soul, even deeper in his heart. He vowed to give her all those things and more.

Following another kiss, he took her hand, prepared to take her to the place that was as much a part of him as she was now. "Okay, sweetheart. Let's go home."

\* \* \* \* \*

*Don't miss the next title in*
DYNASTIES: THE ASHTONS,
*CONDITION OF MARRIAGE*
*by Emilie Rose, available*
*in September from Silhouette Desire.*

**Silhouette**

*Desire*

**brings you an unforgettable
new miniseries from author**

# Linda Conrad

## The Gypsy Inheritance

*A secret legacy unleashes passion…and promises.*

Scandal and seduction go hand in hand as three
powerful men receive unexpected gifts….

# SEDUCTION
# BY THE BOOK

August 2005
Silhouette Desire #1673

# REFLECTED PLEASURES

September 2005
Silhouette Desire #1679

# A SCANDALOUS
# MELODY

October 2005
Silhouette Desire #1684

*Available at your favorite retail outlet.*

# Silhouette Desire

## COMING NEXT MONTH

**#1675 CONDITION OF MARRIAGE—Emilie Rose**
*Dynasties: The Ashtons*
Abandoned by her lover, pregnant Mercedes Ashton turned to her good friend Jared Maxwell for help. Jared offered her a marriage of convenience…that soon flared into unexpected passion. But when the father of Mercedes's unborn child returned, would her bond with Jared be enough to keep their marriage together?

**#1676 TANNER TIES—Peggy Moreland**
*The Tanners of Texas*
Lauren Tanner was determined to get her life back on track…without the assistance of her estranged family. When she hired quiet Luke Jordan, she had no idea the scarred handyman was tied to the Tanners and prepared to use any method necessary—even seduction—to bring Lauren back into the fold.

**#1677 STRICTLY CONFIDENTIAL ATTRACTION—Brenda Jackson**
*Texas Cattleman's Club: The Secret Diary*
Although rancher Mark Hartman's relationship with his attractive secretary, Alison Lind, had always been strictly professional, it changed when he was forced to enlist her aid in caring for his infant niece. Now their business arrangement was venturing into personal—and potentially dangerous—territory….

**#1678 APACHE NIGHTS—Sheri WhiteFeather**
Their attraction was undeniable. But neither police detective Joyce Riggs nor skirting-the-edge-of-the-law Apache Kyle Prescott believed there could be anything more than passion between them. They decided the answer to their dilemma was a no-strings affair. That was their first mistake.

**#1679 REFLECTED PLEASURES—Linda Conrad**
*The Gypsy Inheritance*
Fashion model Merrill Davis-Ross wanted out of the spotlight and had reinvented herself as the new plain-Jane assistant of billionaire Texan Tyson Steele. But her mission to leave her past behind was challenged when Tyson dared to look beyond Merrill's facade to find the real woman underneath.

**#1680 THE RICH STRANGER—Bronwyn Jameson**
*Princes of the Outback*
When fate stranded Australian playboy Rafe Carlisle on her cattle station, usually wary Cat McConnell knew she'd never met anyone like this rich stranger. Because his wild and winning ways tempted her to say yes to night after night of passion, to a temporary marriage—and even to having his baby!

SDCNM0805